AP

C+

THE WIZARD'S TIDE

THE WIZARD'S TIDE

A Story

Frederick Buechner

G.K.HALL &CO.
Boston, Massachusetts
1991

British Commonwealth rights courtesy of
Harriet Wasserman Literary Agency Inc.

Published in Large Print by arrangement with
HarperCollins Publishers.

G.K. Hall Large Print Book Series.

Set in 18 pt. Plantin.

Library of Congress Cataloging-in-Publication Data

Buechner, Frederick, 1926–
    The wizard's tide : a story / Frederick Buechner.
      p. cm.—(G.K. Hall large print book series)
    ISBN 0-8161-5142-3 (lg. print)
    1. Large type books. I. Title.
[PS3552.U35W39 1991]
813′.54—dc20

91-8504

For Bambi and Hatch

one

This is a story about Teddy Schroeder and his sister, Bean, and about some things that happened to them when they were children. It is a mostly true story.

Teddy was grown up when many years later he finally told it. He told it as clearly and simply as he would tell a story to a child—either to a real child or to a child like the one who he felt was holed up inside his grown-up self with a lot of the mysteries about his childhood that he'd never gotten around to solving. He told it because it helped that child inside himself to solve at least some of those mysteries at long last and because—who knows?—maybe it would clear up a few mysteries for other grown-up children too, or even some real children if any of them ever happened to get around to reading it.

Here are some of the mysteries: What was wrong with his father's laughter when he was playing Monopoly, and why was "Well,

well, well" all that his grandfather could say when they arrived in Pittsburgh? Why did Mrs. Lundbeck offer to take them to see the boy who was half crocodile? What was the real reason that his father crawled into the igloo the day after the big snow? What unspoken family law was broken just before he and his sister, Bean, fell asleep on Christmas Eve? All of us have questions like that left over from long ago. It's good to dig them up and take a look at them every once in a while. All of us have things that are healing and hopeful to remember as well as things that are sad and complicated, and one of the main reasons that Teddy told his story is that he enjoyed so much remembering them. Even the sad and complicated ones he enjoyed remembering because they had so many people he loved in them.

There was no television in 1936 because television hadn't been invented yet, and there were no computers or jet airplanes or diet sodas or Frisbees, but there were radios, and there was milk that came in real bottles that clinked when the milkman left them at your back door before you were out of bed in the morning, and there were cars that weren't streamlined the way they are today but looked more like small, square houses moving along on wheels. You didn't have to be rich to have a maid or a cook working for you because they didn't cost very much back then and a lot more people went into that kind of work than they do now.

The president was a man named Franklin D. Roosevelt, who had a cheerful V of a smile and smoked cigarettes in cigarette holders and whom some people hated (like Mr. and Mrs. Schroeder) and other people loved (like Mrs. Lundbeck, who was the Schroeders' cook and helped look after the children). In England they had a brand new king named Edward, whose mother, Queen Mary, wore hats with feathers in them and when she was driven through the streets in her Rolls Royce waved at people backward as if she was waving at herself. There hadn't been a world war for almost twenty years and there wasn't another one until after the things this story is about had finished happening, but there was something called the Depression instead, and it was almost as bad.

Mr. Schroeder sometimes talked about how depressed he felt, and Mrs. Schroeder would say that if he thought *he* felt depressed, someday he should try feeling how *she* felt, but that wasn't the same thing as the Depression.

When Teddy asked Mr. Schroeder what the Depression meant, his answer was, "It means the well's run dry. The party's over." He said, "It means a lot of people have lost a lot of dough. There are families like the Blakes and the Ritters who used to spend summers near us at Sagapac who are lucky now if they can afford an electric fan. Businesses like Grandpa's have either had to close down because they don't have any business any more or have had to fire most of the people who worked for them because they can't pay their salaries any more. Men who used to be millionaires are selling apples on street corners. That's what the Depression means, and if you want my advice, stay clear of it."

Mr. Schroeder had been fired a few weeks before the story begins, and that was part of why he was depressed so often. You could tell he was just by looking at him. He was a handsome young man with plenty of friends, and he was a good tennis player and all the ladies liked to dance with him at parties, but he didn't smile much and even when he did, you could see that his eyes weren't smiling.

Mrs. Schroeder was very pretty. She had

blonde hair and a pleasant sort of sandpapery voice and loved beautiful clothes. She didn't seem to get depressed the way Mr. Schroeder did. But she got mad. She got mad because Mr. Schroeder couldn't find another job and the only money they had to live on was money they'd saved or borrowed from the bank. She got mad because she said he had no get-up-and-go. She got mad because some of her friends had lots of servants to wait on them and all she had was Mrs. Lundbeck to do the cooking and look after Teddy and Bean. And when Mrs. Schroeder got mad she sometimes said such terrible things that she felt sorry about them afterward.

The main trouble with Mrs. Schroeder was that she was so pretty. Most people, if they want other people to be nice to them, have to be nice back. But Mrs. Schroeder didn't. People liked her and were nice to her and wanted to be with her whether she was nice to them or not just because they enjoyed having somebody as pretty as she was around. She never learned to be kind and generous and unselfish because she never had to. She could be all of those things if she felt like it, but she never got the chance to make a habit of it.

Teddy Schroeder was eleven years old.

His hair usually needed cutting, and the bangs came down over his eyes, which were a greenish gray color like wet slate. One of the things he liked best was books. He and Bean had lived in so many different places all their lives that he never had a chance to have the kind of good friends you can have only if you live for a long time in the same place, and so he had books instead. Another reason he liked them so much was not just that they were full of adventures and magic—those were the ones he liked best—but because you could count on books always saying the same thing. A book didn't make you laugh one time you read it and scare you out of your wits the next. It always told the same story the same way, and there were no unpleasant surprises. He especially liked the Oz books, not just *The Wizard of Oz*, which everybody knew, but all the ones that came afterward like *The Road to Oz* and *Ojo in Oz* and *The Lost Princess of Oz* and so on.

In one of them called *The Magic of Oz* there was an old man who knew a magic word you could use for transforming anything into anything else if only you knew how to pronounce it. The word was spelled PYRZQXGL. Teddy understood perfectly well that it was just a fairy tale, but with part of himself he believed in magic and for that reason—even though he felt a little silly doing it—he used to try different ways of pronouncing the magic word just in case. He was apt to do this especially in bed at night when he thought he could tell from Bean's breathing that she was asleep. He would whisper, "Are you asleep, Bean?" and if he got no answer he would try to think up some pronunciations he'd never thought of before and say them under his breath. If he ever got it right, there were all sorts of things he would have liked to be able to do. Like changing the play money in their Monopoly set into real money so they wouldn't have to worry about being poor any more. Or changing all the dresses in his mother's closet into beautiful new ones so she wouldn't get mad so much. Or changing the cocktails his father drank when he came home in the evening from looking for a job into something that didn't make his face feel clammy and cold when he came to kiss him and Bean goodnight.

And there were times when he would have changed Bean herself into something. When he was really fed up with her, he would have changed her into a pebble he could throw into the canal. Or if he only wanted to get her out of his hair for a while, he might just change her into a picture he could hang with its face to the wall till he felt like having her around again.

Bean was two and a half years younger than he was, which doesn't make much difference when you are grown up but makes a big one when one of you is going on eleven and the other is just seven and a half. If anybody asked him if he loved his sister, he would have said yes without even thinking about it. And it was true. He did. But that didn't keep him from being mean to her when he felt like it. Sometimes he would just look her in the eye and start saying something like "widdly widdly widdly wee" to her over and over again in a ghastly kind of baby-talk voice till finally she couldn't stand it any longer and would burst into hysterical shrieks. One time he took a large pink wad of well-chewed bubble gum and, coming up on her unexpectedly from behind, stuck it on the back of her head. It got so gummed up in her hair that even Mrs. Lundbeck, with bits of cotton soaked in Energine, couldn't get rid of it and finally Mrs. Schroeder had to cut it out with a pair of scissors, leaving a horrid bald spot for all the world to see.

One of the worst things he did had to do with a caterpillar. Bean was terrified of caterpillars, and he knew she was. One hot summer day they were walking along the path by the canal—Bean in front and Teddy in back—when he saw crawling up a cattail a great fat green one with black bands and yellow spots on it that looked like one of the three-story-high balloons they have in the Macy's Day parade. "Bean!" he shouted. "Look what I've got for you!" And as soon as she turned, he threw it at her. He must have thrown it a lot harder than he realized because when it hit her, it burst and some of the goo inside got in her mouth. It nearly finished her.

She was a plump little thing. She didn't have much neck to speak of. She had a wide mouth and freckles and a topknot. The topknot was her own idea. She made it fresh every morning with a rubber band, and it stuck right up from the top of her head like a spray. Her mother tried to persuade her at least to tie a ribbon around it, but she didn't like ribbons. She liked it just the way it was.

Even though Teddy was mean to her

sometimes, if he ever got wind that some-body else was mean to her, that somebody was in real trouble. Once at Junior Sports at the Sagapac Field Club, which they both hated, he saw one of the Galt twins snatch off her white tennis hat with "Bean" written on it and then drive her crazy by dangling it just out of reach over her head. Teddy came tearing to her rescue with such a blood-curdling expression on his face that the boy just dropped the hat and walked away. Teddy was mean to his sister, and he also loved her, because that was the way he was.

Mrs. Lundbeck was almost always the one who put them to bed at night. She was a widow who had very little in the way of eye-brows except on her days off, when she drew two dark, squarish ones on with a pencil. She also had false teeth, and once in a while, if she was in the right mood, she would de-light them by popping her teeth out over her lower lip like Dracula. She wasn't the best cook in the world—there were usually lumps in her Cream of Wheat and her string beans were gray—but she was very nice to the chil-dren. After she had them tucked in, she would come turn the lights off and lie down next to one or the other of them, depending

10

on whose turn it was. Then, in the dark, they would all three of them sing a few songs together. Some of the songs they sang were "The Spanish Cavalier," "Do You Ken John Peel," the "Marines' Hymn," and "The Old Rugged Cross." After that, Mrs. Lundbeck would leave, and Teddy and Bean would whisper for a while. One of the things they always whispered about was what they would do when they fell asleep.

There were two possibilities. One was going to Miss Lillywhite's party, which was what their mother said she called going to bed when she was a little girl. And the other was going down the Big Hill, which was something they made up themselves.

If they decided on Miss Lillywhite's party, they would talk about what kind of clothes they would wear to it and who they would find when they got there.

If it was down the Big Hill, they would discuss mainly what kind of sleigh they would go in—a red one? a blue one? with silver trimmings or gold?—and whom they would pick to go with them, like friends or animals or people out of books. It was safe and warm and comfortable in those sleighs because they had roofs on them and fur rugs to put over their knees and windows to look out of. And as they traveled the soft, steep way downward into their dreams, it was always snowing.

two

Their regular house, the one they would go back to when it was time for school, was in New Jersey. Mrs. Schroeder hated New Jersey.

"It's the jumping-off place," she said. Teddy pictured a place so terrible that you'd rather jump off a cliff than stay there. "The only people who live in it are the ones who can't afford to live anywhere else," she said. "Or the ones who don't have the get-up-and-go to clear out." Teddy and Bean both knew whom she meant by that. To show what she thought of it she always called it New Joysey.

They had lived in the New Jersey house only about a year. Before that they had lived somewhere else and before *that* somewhere else still, and so on. Mr. Schroeder was always changing jobs because of the Depression and because he kept trying to find one that would earn him more money to make Mrs. Schroeder happy. Every time he changed his job, they changed the place they lived so that when Teddy and Bean spoke about home they didn't mean one particular house like most people—there had been so many houses—and they didn't mean the New Jersey house, which they'd only been in for such a short time, either. What they probably would have said if anybody had asked them was that home was their mother and father. Home was wherever Mr. and Mrs. Schroeder happened to be living at the time. That's why it scared Teddy so when his mother and father had fights. If someday they got too mad to live together any more, what would happen to him and Bean? If home was gone, where would there be a place for them just to *be?*

The house in New Jersey was nice enough. It was made of stucco and had woods around it and there was a nice lawn in front, but it didn't compare with the lovely big house where Mrs. Schroeder had lived when she was a child. Teddy and Bean knew that house well—it was in a place called Woodland Road, which was a nice part of Pittsburgh, Pennsylvania—because their grandparents, Mrs. Schroeder's mother and father, still lived there, and every once and so often the children were taken to visit them in it. They loved it more than any other house in the

14

world. It had a sleeping porch and a billiard room with a moose's head in it and a library full of beautiful books, which Teddy went on having dreams about until he was almost as old as his grandparents had been. It also had a third floor where the maids lived and where there were rooms full of old steamer trunks with ocean liner labels on them and cedar chests and things that people didn't use any more stored in boxes or hung up in closets.

But the place where this story begins was neither the stucco house in New Jersey nor the big house in Pittsburgh but another house altogether, near the canal in a town on Long Island called Sagapac. This was the gray shingle house that for several years the Schroeders had rented for the summer. It was a little too near a small gas station to suit Mrs. Schroeder, but by the porch it had a honeysuckle bush that buzzed with bees all through July and August and a wide green lawn that stretched down to the water and a dock where Mr. Schroeder tied up the row-boat he used when he went out crabbing. There were rag rugs on the floors, and lots of sand that got tracked in from the beach, and muslin curtains that when the breeze ballooned them out into the room you could see had been mended a lot, and sheets that felt damp when you slid your bare feet in between them at night.

Right next to the Schroeders lived the children's other grandparents—their Schroeder grandmother, who was fat enough so that when she sat in her chair crocheting she could set out her spools of silk and needles on her bosom like a shelf, and their Schroeder grandfather, who had a drooping moustache and watery eyes and usually held a pipe clenched between his teeth. Their house had a wide porch all along the canal side where in the evenings Grandpa Schroeder shook up the cocktails. It also had a butler's pantry with a metal sink where Grandma Schroeder would put an apron on over her dress and take a pair of scissors and arrange the flowers—zinnias or black-eyed Susans or rambler roses, which Rosa and Anna, the German maids, would gather for her when they went out for their weekly walk on Sunday afternoons. It was his Schroeder grandparents who were to give Teddy a party on his eleventh birthday, and that is where the story really begins.

Mrs. Schroeder had a theory about birthday parties. "You invite exactly as many children as there are years in the birthday," she said. "For a three year old, three is plenty, let me tell you. And after sixteen, you're on your own."

"How come you didn't invite ten people when I was ten then?" Teddy asked. He didn't remember exactly how many she had invited except that he was sure there were more than ten plus a tired-looking man in a clown suit who kept saying dumb things like "Howdydoodlydoo" and making his false ears flap.

"That's because Daddy had a job then and we were feeling flush," she said. So eleven was the number that was invited.

There were the Galt twins, who ran around bare at the beach club bath house and snapped you with wet sandy towels that left red marks where they hit. Their parents were friends of Teddy's parents, and that is the only reason they were there. And there was Roger Mittendorf, who lived in another one of the houses on the canal and had a father, he told them, who spanked him sometimes with a strap and a skinny mother with orange hair who Bean said looked like a carrot. And Sally Hartman, who was Bean's best friend and when the three of them played together never made a fuss about Teddy's always being the king but was

17

perfectly willing to be a slave and do anything she was asked to. And Virginia Miller, who was almost fourteen and had hair so long she could sit on it and was very ladylike and didn't call Teddy Teddy the way everybody else did but Ted, like his father. And a few others.

It was to be a masquerade party because that was what Teddy wanted. If you couldn't really change things into other things by some sort of magic like PYRZQXGL, you could at least change yourself by dressing up like somebody else.

Teddy decided to dress up like a drum major because that was the costume he'd been given out of the F. A. O. Schwartz Christmas catalogue the year before. It had a scarlet jacket with gold buttons down the front and a tall busby hat and a silver sword that buckled around the waist. The only costume Bean had was an old Felix the Cat one left over from some earlier Halloween, but she'd gotten too big, especially around the middle, to wear it any more so Mrs. Schroeder had taken her to Woolworth's and let her pick out another one. The one she picked was a fairy princess costume. It had a gauzy skirt that went all the way to the floor and wings sewed on the back and was made of some sort of sleazy cloth that smelled like medicine. It came with a magic wand and a crown that had feelers sticking out of it.

Bean thought it was very beautiful when she first tried it on, but as soon as Teddy saw it, he thought it was awfully funny.

"You know what it makes you look like, don't you?" he said.

She was standing in front of the long mirror on the inside of Mrs. Schroeder's closet door with the wand in her hand and the crown on her head and Mrs. Lundbeck hovering over her with pins sticking out of her mouth.

"What?" Bean said.

"It makes you look just like a caterpillar," Teddy said, and it got him laughing so hard that tears started running down his cheeks.

"It does not either," Bean said, but she knew exactly what he meant. The dress was a sort of caterpillary green color, and there were the feelers coming out of the crown.

"Yes, it does," Teddy said.

"Doesn't."

"Does a million times."

"Doesn't *infinity*," Bean said.

She won that round because she knew that infinity was as many times as you can get, but Teddy won everything else because she

19

ended up saying she was going to take the costume off and never put it on again ever.

Then there was a terrible fuss. Since the party was to be that very afternoon, there was no time to find anything else for her, and when Mrs. Schroeder got wind of it, she said they couldn't afford to throw money out of the window like that even if there was time. She was mad at Bean, but she was even madder at Teddy because he had started it.

"As if I didn't have enough on my mind!" she said to him. "Just wait till I tell Daddy when he gets home."

It always made Teddy's scalp feel cold when she said that. Mr. Schroeder never did much about it when she told him things. He was a gentle sort of man who had never spanked either of his children even with his bare hand let alone with a strap like Roger Mittendorf's father. But just to hear his mother say she'd tell his father scared Teddy more than almost anything else. When he and Bean fought, that was bad enough. And when he and his mother fought, that was just so much worse. And then if his mother went ahead and told his father and all his father did was just shake his head and give him a disgusted look, that would probably end up by making them fight with each other too. And that was the worst thing of all, and every time it happened it made him afraid that the very ground they were standing on would split apart like an earthquake and they would all be swallowed up into it.

"I was just teasing, Bean," he said. "I didn't mean it, honestly. It's just those feelers. If you don't wear the crown, it will look just fine. I promise you."

He lifted the crown off her head, and she turned to look at herself in the mirror again. Then he fluffed up the gauzy wings a little and raised the hand she was holding the wand in up into the air so it looked as if she was about to cast a magic spell.

She turned this way and that way in front of the mirror and finally said, "OK then. I'll wear it if I've got to, but I won't wear that stupid crown again ever in my whole life."

And then just when Teddy thought everything was going to be all right, Mrs. Schroeder said, "The crown's the cutest part of the whole thing, and now you say you won't wear it. That's the last straw."

It was an expression he hated. When the last straw was gone, who could say what horror would be next?

Mrs. Lundbeck came to the rescue. "Oh she'll wear it, Mrs. Schroeder," she said.

"She'll wear it when the time comes and be the prettiest girl at the party."

Only when the time came, she wouldn't.

Teddy was all dressed up in his drum major suit, and Mrs. Schroeder had put on her lipstick and pearls, and they were just about to leave in time to be at the grandparents' house before the first guests started arriving. Then suddenly Mrs. Lundbeck noticed that the crown she had set down on a table for a moment was missing. Everybody knew that Bean had done something with it, but she refused to say what. She just stood there smelling of medicine with her mouth clamped grimly shut.

"She has hidden it somewhere in this room," Mrs. Schroeder said. And then she said to Bean, "Well, I just give up. If you want to go bareheaded and have everybody think how silly you look, then it's your hard luck."

"I see it," Mrs. Lundbeck said.

In a moment she was down on her hands and knees reaching under the couch. Then she gave a little yelp. She had banged her glasses on the couch leg. One of the lenses was cracked, and there was a bloody scratch over her eye. She wobbled a bit when she got up on her feet again and dabbed at the scratch with her handkerchief, smudging one of the eyebrows she had drawn on for the party.

She was a good sport about it and didn't blame Bean, but Bean felt awful anyhow, and Teddy knew that if he hadn't said she looked like a caterpillar, the whole thing would never have happened. Mrs. Schroeder said it was the Pink Limit. So all in all, you'd never have guessed that they were going to a birthday party if you'd seen the way they trailed across the grass.

They went single file and nobody talked to anybody else. Mrs. Lundbeck went last, carrying the crown with the feelers sticking out, which wobbled as she picked her way carefully along because she couldn't see where she was going very well thanks to the cracked lens in her glasses.

three

Teddy was always glad that his birthday came in the summer. Poor Bean's was in November, when people were still either just getting over Thanksgiving or just starting to get ready for Christmas. She had a party and presents like everybody else, of course, but they were so squeezed in between other things that you hardly noticed. In summers, on the other hand, people were always looking for ways to have fun and they were willing to go to any lengths to have it.

Even Grandpa Schroeder. He was one of the ones who had lost his business because of the Depression, so he didn't do much any more. In the morning he would sit around the house smoking his pipe, and in the afternoon he might go off with a friend and a caddy to play a little golf, and in the evening when the sun was beginning to set he would always start making cocktails out on the piazza, which was what they called a porch in those days. He made them in a silver shaker,

which he held in both hands and shook vig-
orously up and down near one of his ears
with his head cocked slightly to one side as
if he could tell when they were ready from
the velvety rattle of the ice cubes inside.
When he poured them out, they had a sort
of pale orangey color to them and a little
creamy foam on top.

But this day was different, because for
Teddy's birthday Grandpa was given the job
of setting things up for musical chairs on the
lawn. He got Rosa the maid to carry the
chairs out and help him line them up with
one facing one way and the next facing the
other way. Then he himself carried out the
victrola, which was the kind of record player
they had back then. You wound it up with
a crank that stuck out of one side, and it
had two kinds of needles you could use—
either a steel one that lasted the longest but
sounded harsh and scratchy or a wooden one
that sounded much nicer and softer but wore
out in almost no time. Grandpa Schroeder
had a gimpy leg, so it took him quite a while
to get all this ready. Then he put on a pair
of white flannel trousers, a blue blazer, and
a lopsided bow tie and went and sat out on
one of the canvas lawn chairs, taking a highball with him to help him recover from all

his exertions while he waited for things to start up. Grandma Schroeder called through the screen door that she didn't want him to drink more than one, but he pretended he didn't hear her.

Almost everybody was scared of Grandma Schroeder, especially when she looked you in the eye and started talking to you with the word *say*. "Say," she would say to Teddy. "You should be out playing games with the other boys more instead of always sitting around somewhere with your nose in a book. When your father was your age, he could outswim boys twice his size." Or to Mrs. Schroeder she would say, "Say, you must think you're married to a millionaire to spend as much money as that new pink evening dress must have cost."

She had a high-pitched fat lady's laugh that came out in little squeals, and she could be very jolly and fun to be with if she felt like it. She also gave everybody wonderful Christmas presents. But she told you exactly what she thought of you whether it was pleasant to hear or not, and nobody dared talk back to her. The reason they didn't was not only that she was so strong and so fierce but also that she was the one member of the family who still had lots of money.

Her father had left it to her, and she had kept it in banks or invested it in real estate so when the Depression came it didn't really bother her very much. She had two other sons besides Teddy's father—Uncle Jeff, who was very smart, and Uncle Phil, who was very funny—and they and their wives were as scared of her as everybody else. They'd roll their eyes and make faces at each other behind her back when she was on a rampage, but only on very rare occasions did they dare to do any more than that.

She had Rosa in a frenzy all morning blowing up balloons to hang around the piazza, and carpet-sweeping everywhere, and putting both the extra leaves in the dining room table, and setting it with favors and poppers and paper hats and all the rest of it. She made Anna, who was Rosa's sister and did the cooking, spend hours decorating the huge birthday cake with things like baseball bats and footballs and tennis rackets, which she squeezed out of a cone full of frosting. Grandma Schroeder chose those kinds of things for the decoration not because Teddy liked them but because they were things she thought he ought to like. Her own boys had liked them, and it was the way boys were supposed to be.

The party went off the way parties usually do. The Galt twins cheated at Pin the Tail on the Donkey. They complained that Mrs. Schroeder had tied their blindfolds on too tight, and when she loosened them a little everybody knew they could see, though when Roger Mittendorf said so, Peter Galt threatened to punch him in the nose and Bean said how could he punch him in the nose if he couldn't see where his nose was.

It was Bean, too, who won musical chairs. She had long since forgotten about the crown business. Grandpa Schroeder worked the victrola. He kept the lid of it raised so they couldn't see when he was going to raise the arm to stop it, and the record he put on was "The March of the Wooden Soldiers," because he said with his bad leg he walked as though he was made of wood himself. Bean and Virginia Miller were the last two children left. Virginia was gotten up like Alice in Wonderland, with a ribbon tied around her long hair and a frilly starched apron over her old-fashioned dress. She and Bean ended up in the last chair at so close to the same instant that it was impossible to say which of them had gotten there first, but Virginia was so polite and ladylike that she said Bean had, and so it was to Bean that her grandfather handed the prize. It was a jar of Schrafft's sourballs, and he first almost handed her his third highball by mistake, which made everybody laugh.

They sat down to eat at about five thirty as they'd planned, and the food was what everybody had at birthday parties in those days, which was creamed chicken in patty shells and mashed potatoes and green peas. A friend of Teddy's named Beaver Murphy, the son of the man who ran the garage that was too near their house for Mrs. Schroeder's liking, started putting peas in his blower and shooting them at people across the table, but when nobody else was looking, Mrs. Lundbeck popped her teeth out at him and after that he didn't do it again.

Teddy was a shy boy and didn't usually like parties much, but he liked this one a lot. He liked especially the scarlet jacket with the gold buttons he was wearing. It made him look like a king, and kings were what interested him more than almost anything else. He loved reading about them in books, kings like the King of the Golden River and King Arthur and Ruggedo the Gnome King, and also real kings like the ones who got their pictures in the rotogravure section of the newspapers with their beards and race horses

29

and tall silk hats, or the long-ago ones like bad King Richard, who had his little nephews murdered in the Tower, or fat King Louis, whose head was cut off by the guillotine. He would have liked to be a king himself when he grew up because then he could make everybody behave right, or if they didn't he could tell them they might end up on the guillotine themselves. He wished his father had been a king because then he would have been sure to be one himself.

He also liked sitting next to Virginia Miller, whose hair, when she leaned over to whisper something in his ear, smelled of Conti Castille shampoo. But maybe what he liked most of all was not only that everybody had on their best clothes but also—except for Beaver getting a little overexcited and the Galt twins peeking out from under their blindfolds—that all of them were on their best behavior. You knew that nobody was going to start fighting and everything was going to turn out just the way parties should.

He was thinking about all this and enjoying himself when the kitchen door swung open, and there stood Rosa in her best wine-colored uniform with the lace cap and apron. She was carrying a silver platter with the big birthday cake ablaze with candles on it, and behind her Anna was peering in at all of them over her sister's shoulder. For a second or two there was a hush before they started singing "Happy Birthday" to him, and during that hush he heard his mother speak to his grandmother. They were standing over by the sideboard watching all the goings-on.

"Ted swore he'd be here in time for the cake," his mother said. "I just think it's too mean."

And his grandmother said, "I just hope he hasn't had an accident driving out from the city. Such awful things happen to people."

So while they all sang to him and Rosa walked slowly around the table with the candles lighting her face from below and set the cake down in front of him so he could blow them out, he could feel his stomach turn upside down inside him and the top of his head go cold as ice. The Ted they were talking about was his father, of course. His grandfather was Ted too, and Teddy himself was Ted the Third.

It was almost dark before his father finally arrived. The guests had long since gone home. Mrs. Schroeder told Mrs. Lundbeck she might as well take the evening off because there was no supper to cook and it was obvious *she* wasn't going anywhere. Grandpa Schroeder urged his daughter-in-law to stay and have a cocktail with them. Grandma Schroeder said she didn't see how anybody could think of cocktails at a time like this and if Ted wasn't back in a half an hour she was going to call the police. So Mrs. Schroeder stayed and smoked a lot of cigarettes. All this happened before anybody thought that smoking was bad for your health, though the chances are she would have smoked a lot of them anyway.

Teddy and Bean were out on the lawn trying to catch fireflies in the dusk with their paper hats when they recognized their father's car coming up the driveway. It was an old second-hand Pierce Arrow with a cracked rear window that he had bought to go to work in when he still had a job, leaving the good car for Mrs. Schroeder and the children. The headlights weren't turned on though it was almost too dark to see, and instead of stopping at the usual place next to the garage, he kept going till the front of the car was up on the lawn nosing into a lilac bush.

As soon as he got out of the car, he squatted down on his haunches waiting for Teddy to run up and throw himself into his arms.

"How's my old Skeezix?" Mr. Schroeder said, laughing, and then gave Teddy what the children called one of his hard kisses. A hard kiss was when he buried his whole face against them and snorted into their cheeks and necks and tickled them with his whiskers till they got laughing so hard they could hardly breathe. "Go see what I've got in the car for you," he said and then picked Bean up under the arms and held her way up in the air over him. It turned out there wasn't anything for Teddy in the car because Mr. Schroeder must have forgotten to put it in before he left the city.

Mrs. Schroeder by now was standing in the driveway with the porch light behind her making it look as if her hair was on fire. "Well, I should think you'd be ashamed of yourself," she said.

"I've got good news, darling," he said. He had put Bean back down again and was leaning with one elbow against the Pierce Arrow.

"Dahling, dahling," she said, making fun of the way he pronounced it with his New York accent.

Grandma Schroeder had come out onto

the piazza. "I don't know how you can be so cruel," she said. "I thought you were lying dead in a ditch."

Teddy was afraid that she was going to notice where the car was parked and make an awful fuss, but luckily it was too dark. So his father said he was sorry he was late, and Grandma Schroeder just made some little hurt sound which meant that at least for the time being that would be the end of it. Then Teddy and Bean and their parents went back to their own house.

When they got there, Mr. Schroeder was very happy and excited. He told Mrs. Schroeder that the reason he was so late was that he had had a really lucky break in the city that day and he wanted to take her down to the Sagapac Field Club or somewhere to celebrate.

He was sitting on the couch with Teddy on one of his knees and Bean on the other, his arms around them both. He let on that Bean's topknot was tickling his nose and pretended to have a sneezing fit. That made Bean almost giggle herself right off his lap, and even Teddy couldn't help smiling, though on the inside he didn't feel much like it because he was afraid there was going to be trouble.

"You've done enough celebrating already. You should just smell your breath," Mrs. Schroeder said. "You're as bad as your father and thirty years younger. What you need is a cup of black coffee and a good swift kick in the pants."

But Mr. Schroeder was in such a good mood and he looked so tan and handsome in the gabardine suit he went job hunting in that Mrs. Schroeder's voice began to soften a little. Teddy heard it and thought that maybe everything would be all right after all.

Then Mr. Schroeder made his wife sit down on the couch between his two children, and he stood in the middle of the room and pretended he was a school teacher explaining the day's lesson to them.

"Now over here," he said, pointing to himself, "is Ted Schroeder. He's a good-looking young fella with an awful pretty wife he doesn't half deserve and he darn well knows it. He's also got two cute kids. One of them has a topknot that makes her look like Zip the What-Is-It Girl and the other one can be a real sourpuss sometimes, but their Daddy loves them both like the dickens anyhow so that's all there is to say about that."

Then he walked over to another part of the room near the window and crouched down part way to make himself look shorter. He lost his balance doing it and had to catch hold of a curtain to keep from falling.

"Now over *here* is a little shrimp named Joseph Armbruster Perkins, known as Perky. Perky the turkey," he said and giggled. "Perky went to college with young Ted over there, and Perky's not much to look at and some people say he sews his underwear on in the winter and doesn't take it off again till spring, but Perky's got one thing that Ted doesn't have and that is gray matter. If you don't know what gray matter is, I'll tell you. It's brains. Perky may be a turkey, but he's a damned smart turkey." Then he slapped his arms up and down and kept on saying, "Gobble, gobble, gobble" with such a silly expression on his face that finally even Mrs. Schroeder had to laugh.

As soon as he saw that she wasn't quite as mad at him as she had been, he stopped being silly and got very serious. He came over and sat down on the floor next to where she was on the couch. He took her hand and kept on holding it in his all the time he was talking.

Perky had come up with a great invention,

Mr. Schroeder said. He had invented a kind of glass that could stand as much heat as metal or ceramics. You could put it in the oven or pour boiling water on it, and it wouldn't so much as crack. This was before anybody else had invented such a thing, of course, and he said that it would revolution- ize the whole glass industry. The point was this, he said, and his voice got very quiet as he said it. Perky wanted to start a company to manufacture the stuff, and he wanted Mr. Schroeder to be vice president. All he had to do in return was invest a little money in it now to help get it started and inside of a year they'd be making millions. They wouldn't have to live in New Jersey any more but could move to some nice town in West- chester or Connecticut. They could afford to buy a summer house of their own instead of renting the one they were in at the mo- ment. Mrs. Schroeder wouldn't have to worry about pinching pennies any more but could have anything she wanted.

Teddy could see in his mother's face how much she wanted to believe him. Her lips were slightly parted as though she was saying all over again to some invisible person the same words that Mr. Schroeder was saying to her. Her eyes were bright with hopefulness, and she looked so pretty sitting there with the lamplight glinting in her hair and on her pearls that Teddy thought it was the way she would look if his father really was a king and she was his royal queen. But even as he was thinking that, he saw a shadow flit across her face.

"Teddy, where in the world are you ever going to get money to invest in anything?" she said. "You know how broke we are as it is." She usually called him Ted, not Teddy, but this was not a usual moment.

Mr. Schroeder laid one finger lightly across her lips. Her name was Constance but her little girl name had been Cici, and that was what he called her now. Most people called her Connie.

"Cici," he said, "you don't have to worry about that." And when she started to say something in spite of his finger on her lips, he spoke in such a solemn way that Teddy felt it was like hearing President Roosevelt make a speech over the radio. She couldn't help but listen to what he had to say.

He said that Grandma Schroeder would lend him the money. He knew he could talk her into it. And he could borrow something on his life insurance if any more was needed. A few thousand dollars was all it would take, and then they would start making the marvelous new glass. Before you could wink an eye they would pay everything back and be on Easy Street.

As soon as he finished, he leaned forward until his head touched Mrs. Schroeder's head. For a few moments nobody said anything. The only sound in the room was the tick-tock, tick-tock of the clock on the mantle.

"We're going to be rich, Teddy. Daddy said so himself," Bean said. It was later that night when they were about to go to sleep. They had put themselves to bed because Mrs. Lundbeck had gone to the movies and Mr. and Mrs. Schroeder were downstairs playing music on the victrola and talking.

"I sure hope so," Teddy said.

"And we'll have a chauffeur like Paul to drive us anywhere we want to go," Bean said. Paul was the chauffeur that Grandma and Grandpa Schroeder had when they went back to New York for the winter. "Everything will be so lovely and nice."

Teddy didn't say so to Bean, but he thought to himself that the loveliest and nicest thing he could remember for a long time had already happened. It had happened downstairs when his father's suntanned forehead and his mother's golden hair had touched just for a moment. For as long as that moment lasted he believed that there was no sad or scary thing in all the world that could ever touch any of them.

"Miss Lillywhite's party?" Bean asked sleepily.

"Yes," Teddy said, but he was so sleepy himself that they didn't bother to talk about what sort of clothes they would wear to it or who they hoped they might find when they got there.

four

The children were woken up the next morning by the sound of ducks quacking as Rosa fed them. She would take the toast crusts left over from breakfast and scatter them into the canal from the dock. Sometimes two ducks would get the same crust in both their beaks at once and make a great racket fighting to see which would end up with it. Sometimes they would come waddling up onto the lawn and do their eating there, dropping their white feathers all over the grass.

It was a beautiful sunny day with a blue sky and not a single cloud in it. There was a whiff of low tide in the air and a little honeysuckle from the bush by the porch steps. Bean felt so good that she did something she liked to do every once in a while. She jumped out of bed and stood by the window in just her underdrawers. Then she puffed out her stomach and blew out her cheeks as far as they would go to make herself look like a balloon. When she was just about to burst and her face was turning crimson, she would jab her finger into her lips with a loud explosion of breath and then go careening all over the room, bouncing off walls and running into furniture and batting against doors until she finally collapsed on the floor in a limp tangle. All the time she was doing this, Teddy lay on top of the covers in his pajamas and crowed like a rooster with his legs in the air.

It was a Saturday, and Mrs. Schroeder's main birthday present was going to be to take Teddy into New York to see a matinee of *The Mikado.* He had never been to a Gilbert and Sullivan operetta before, and since the famous Doyly Carte company was in town that summer, she thought it would be a good time for it. She wasn't going to take Bean because she said Bean was too young, and Teddy wasn't too happy about that. In some ways he liked being his mother's pet, but in other ways there were times when it seemed sort of sad and lonely. To make Bean feel better he told her while they were getting dressed that *The Mikado* was supposed to be very long and boring and he wished he wasn't going himself. It was all about some old man walking up and down in an empty room trying to decide about something, he said. By the time he was through he'd done such a good job of it that Bean had almost decided that she was the lucky one to be staying home. Then when Mr. Schroeder came down for breakfast, she was sure of it.

He had on his navy blue polo shirt and a pair of khaki pants with the legs rolled up to his calves. His hair was still wet and plastered flat from the shower, and he wore it parted straight down the middle the way men used to. He said to Bean that while the two city slickers went off to New York, he and she were going to have some fun of their own right there. How would she like to go crabbing, he asked her. They would get Mrs. Lundbeck to make them some deviled ham sandwiches and they would take a couple of long-handled nets and then head off down the canal in their rowboat and see what they could see.

Bean thought it was a wonderful idea, and by the time Teddy and Mrs. Schroeder were ready to drive down to the train station, she and her father were already leaving the house with their lunch and the two nets.

"Don't forget to ask your mother about you know what," she called down the stairs.

"It'll be a pushover," he said.

Once they were on their way, it was fun

43

being just the two of them, Teddy thought. His mother didn't look like a carrot the way Mrs. Mittendorf did. She didn't even look like a mother the way the mothers of most of his friends did with their frizzy hair and brown faces. She looked like a movie star. Her hair was shiny and soft and she didn't wear too much lipstick like some of them. Just the way she held her shoulders when she walked, anybody could see she was somebody special. He had the feeling there was nothing she couldn't do if she once set her mind to it, and if Carol Lombard or Haile Selassie or Babe Ruth should happen to turn up someday, she would know just as well how to talk with them as she would with Little Mrs. Joe, the dwarf lady who sold hot hogs at the public beach, or with him or Bean or Grandpa Schroeder or anybody else. He was very proud of her.

Before trains went as fast as they do nowadays, they let you open the windows if you wanted to, and Teddy and his mother opened theirs as they went rattling along through the small towns and potato fields of the flat Long Island countryside. The seats were covered with slippery varnished straw, and since the one in front of them didn't have anybody in it, they turned it around so it was facing them and they could put their feet up.

Mrs. Schroeder was in a very good mood. She told him about things she and her friends used to do when she was a girl growing up in Pittsburgh. Sometimes they would call up the tobacco store and ask the clerk if he had Prince Albert in a can, she said, and then if he answered yes, they would ask him to please let him out. Or she would hail a streetcar and when it stopped to pick her up, she would put her foot up on the step that came down when the door opened, tie her shoe, and then walk away saying, "Thank you very much." She also told him how they had a nurse named Sadie Sorg who could laugh like a man, and once in a while they would get her to laugh like that in the ladies' room, and he couldn't even imagine the commotion *that* caused, she said.

Mrs. Schroeder had a laugh that came tumbling out the way a wave comes tumbling over the beach, but just when you thought that was the end of it, there would be another wave still, and Teddy loved laughing with her. She had brought them each a Hershey bar in her purse for lunch, and while they ate them, she told him about some of the beaux she used to have when she was young.

45

She told him about Alfonse Biedemaier, a Swiss cavalry officer who taught her how to ride by sliding a broom handle through her crooked elbows and having her hold it clamped so tight to her back that she learned to sit straight as a cavalry officer herself. She also told him about Barry Simpson who had a stutter and got so frustrated trying to say something to her during a winter sleigh ride once that he ended by picking her up in his arms and throwing her into a snowdrift. And about Scotty Vaningen, who when he came to call on her one day stepped through her father's straw hat by mistake while he was hanging his coat up in the closet and then didn't dare come out for hours for fear that her father would see him and find out what he'd done.

Even as he was laughing with her, Teddy thought about his father and how he was the beau that his mother had finally decided to get married to. He thought of his father and Bean out in the rowboat together peering down into the muddy green water for the flicker of a crab swimming up toward the surface, and for a moment or two he felt a flicker of something swimming up in him and thought that maybe he ought to be back there in the rowboat with them and not taking the train to New York with his mother.

"Today my beau is named Teddy Bear," she was saying, brushing his shaggy bangs out of his eyes. She leaned over and kissed him on top of his head.

Almost the best part of *The Mikado*, he thought, were the costumes. The kimonos with their trailing sleeves and enormous sashes in every marvelous Oz book color he had ever seen were so brilliant in the dazzling lights that it almost made his eyes ache to look at them. The Mikado himself wore a black hat with a long black tongue that curled far out over his head from behind, and Katisha's piles of lacquered hair were stuck full of knitting needles that had tiny Japanese lanterns hanging from them, and Yum Yum had little black smudges painted high up on her forehead for eyebrows and sang "The Sun and I" in a robe as white as the whitest snow embroidered all over with silver moons and stars that glittered every time she moved. Mrs. Schroeder thought she was the best one of them all, whereas Teddy preferred the Lord High Executioner, a slender, acrobatic man who scrambled half way up one of the tall gold curtains that hung tied back at the side of the stage. He also loved the big fans they all carried in their sleeves and the graceful way they flicked them open and clapped them shut and could make them flutter or swoop through the air like giant butterflies.

During the intermission they each had some prickly tasting orange drink, which left them thirstier than they were before they drank it, and when they were going back to their seats, Mrs. Schroeder leaned down and whispered into his ear, "Teddy, look. See who that is sitting there on the left holding her chin," and who did it turn out to be but Mrs. Eleanor Roosevelt, the president's wife. She gave him a friendly smile as he walked by trying not to stare too hard at her, and he saw those famous buck teeth she had that everybody made fun of in jokes and cartoons. He thought how excited Bean would have been if she'd been there and wondered whether it would make her sad to think what she'd missed if he told her about it when they got home.

"We've got a little time before we have to catch our train," Mrs. Schroeder said when they stepped out of the theater after it was all over. "I thought it would be fun to stop in at the Biltmore for a sundae or something. They've got a cute little coffee shop there, and we might run into an old friend of mine I think may be in town this week."

They decided to walk to save taxi money, and it wasn't all that far anyhow. New York looked a lot the way it does now except for the people. Even though it was a warm summer day nobody except little children wore short pants into the city then, and most of the men had jackets and ties on and most of the women wore silk stockings and hats and carried purses. There were still organ grinders around, and one of them was standing in front of the public library where the stone lions are as Teddy and his mother walked by. The monkey had a red felt cap with a pom-pom on it tied under his chin, and he took the penny out of Teddy's hand with his leathery fingers and dropped it into the organ grinder's tin cup as if he understood exactly what he was doing and would be happy to explain it to you if you asked him.

There were green double-decker buses on Fifth Avenue. Some of them were closed in and some were open and you got to the top deck by taking a steep stairway that went up from the rear platform. You didn't pay your money as you got on the way you did on the other buses, but a conductor came to you after you were sitting down and held out a small chromium counting machine with a slot in it that you were supposed to stick your dime in. A dime was all it cost to ride a Fifth Avenue bus in those days. The machine was so powerful that it seemed to suck the coin right out of your fingers. The other buses were only a nickle.

Mrs. Lundbeck made the children squirm with embarrassment once when she took them for a ride on a bus. When the conductor held his machine out to her, she refused to put her dime in it. She said it made it too easy for them to cheat you that way, and she would have none of it. If the man wanted her dime, he could reach out and take it with his hand like anybody else. What he did with it after that was none of her business. When Teddy and Bean asked her later how she thought the man could have cheated her, she wouldn't explain it to them. She had circles of pink rouge on her cheeks that day in addition to the day-off eyebrows, and she wouldn't explain that either.

Mrs. Schroeder said there was a famous clock at the Biltmore Hotel where people met their friends, and sure enough when they got there, there it was at the top of the steps you had to walk up to get to the lobby. It wasn't very big and didn't look famous at all. There was a bench underneath the clock, and one of the people sitting on it was the person Mrs. Schroeder had said she thought might be in the city that day. He was a tall man with white crooked teeth and eyebrows that met over his nose and a friendly smile. She said he was an old friend from Pittsburgh named Mr. MacFarland, and he reached out and shook Teddy by the hand. He and Mrs. Schroeder kissed each other hello, and she called him Mac. He said she was looking as great as always, and she said he was looking great too, and they both laughed.

In the coffee shop Teddy had a butterscotch sundae with sauce so thick that it left a sticky thread trailing back to the dish when you took a spoonful of it and you had to break the thread with your fingers and try to wind it around the spoon so you wouldn't get it all over you as you put it in your mouth. His mother and Mr. MacFarland just had iced tea.

They talked a lot about people Teddy had never heard of, and he didn't pay much attention to it. He was busy with his sundae and thinking about *The Mikado* and wondering if Bean and his father were back from their crabbing yet and what they were doing

51

right then. He thought too about how much his mother had had to pay for the train both ways and the theater tickets and the orange drinks, and it made him feel a little sad and lonesome inside knowing they couldn't afford it and that Bean wasn't there winding butterscotch sauce around her spoon too.

His mother and Mr. MacFarland had laughed a lot when they first sat down, but they were talking quietly now, he on one side of the table and she on the other side, with their heads bent forward. His mother was saying, "I don't know how much longer I can take it, Mac," and Mr. MacFarland patted the back of her hand and said, "Soldiers aren't the only ones who deserve medals."

They both lit cigarettes on one match, which Mr. MacFarland held cupped in his large hand. Then Mr. MacFarland asked Teddy if he liked baseball, and when Teddy was too embarrassed to say he didn't, his mother said it for him.

"That makes two of us then," Mr. MacFarland said, and all three of them laughed.

When they were finished Mr. MacFarland paid the check and took them down to Penn Station in a yellow Checker cab. Mrs. Schroeder said she wouldn't let him go all the way down to where the Long Island trains left from, so while the taxi waited, he got out and said goodbye to them right there in front of the great marble columns that made even Mr. MacFarland look about three feet high.

He didn't kiss Mrs. Schroeder goodbye. He put both his hands on her shoulders, looked down into her face, and said, "You always know how you can get hold of me if you want me." She just nodded without saying anything. When he was back in the cab again, he reached his hand out through the window, and she reached out and touched it with hers. Then he was off.

Just before they pulled into the station at Sagapac, Mrs. Schroeder took hold of Teddy's chin and turned his head around to face her.

"Promise me something, Teddy," she said.

He knew it wasn't going to be something like "Promise me you'll never cross the street without looking both ways," or anything of that sort. It was something she wanted him to do just for her sake, and she had the same kind of pleading look in her eyes that Bean had sometimes.

"Don't mention to Daddy about Mr. MacFarland," Mrs. Schroeder said.

"How come?" Teddy asked.

"Because I ask you," his mother said. "And because Daddy never liked him. It would lead to a fight if he knew."

"OK," Teddy said. It made him feel awful, but fights were more awful still.

When they got home, Bean was in the living room though there was still plenty of sunshine outside. She was sitting on the floor with an empty beer bottle trying to see how many toothpicks she could pile on top of the neck. People who were really good at it could get hundreds.

"We caught seven crabs," she said. "They're swimming around in the pail if you want to go see them. Daddy got five and I got two."

"Where's Daddy now?" Mrs. Schroeder asked.

"The Pierce Arrow's busted," Bean said. "I think he's over at the garage seeing if they can fix it."

She didn't even ask Teddy how *The Mikado* was. If she asked later, he decided he'd wait till his mother wasn't around and then say it was stupid and boring. That would make another fib about what had happened

54

in New York that day. He didn't like telling fibs, but sometimes you had to do all sorts of things you didn't like just to keep everything peaceful.

It was a little like piling toothpicks on top of a bottle. If you weren't very careful about the way you did it, the whole works would fall apart and go tumbling.

five

The next day was Sunday, and it was just as beautiful as the day before only hotter. What made it beautiful to Teddy, though, was not so much the weather as the fact that everybody woke up that morning feeling happy.

The reason wasn't hard to find. As soon as Mr. Schroeder had gotten back from the garage the day before, he told them that his mother had said she would lend him two thousand dollars to put into the new glass business that was going to make them rich. This was in the days when all it cost to mail a letter was three cents, and you could get a haircut for a quarter, and a big meal at a restaurant for what you'd pay nowadays for a milkshake, and a car for not much more than the price of a good color TV. When Teddy and Bean were children, in other words, two thousand dollars was a lot of money.

His mother wasn't very enthusiastic about lending it. She nibbled at her fingernails when things bothered her, and all the while Teddy's father was telling her about Perky and his miraculous new invention, she had sat on the piazza looking at him over her knuckles and nibbling.

"I guess I can afford to lend the money if I have to, but I certainly can't afford to throw it down the drain," she said. "I just hope you know what you're doing, Ted. You're much too big-hearted and easygoing. That's why people are always taking advantage of you. It's why you lost your job when men who haven't been there half as long as you still have theirs. You've got to be tough if you want to get anywhere in this world. My father was tough, and it's only thanks to him we're not in the poor house today."

Grandpa Schroeder was pottering around nearby, trimming the honeysuckle with a pair of garden shears, and she spoke her last words loudly enough so he would get the point. The point was that if *he* was all they had to depend on, they would be in the poor house for sure. But if he got it, he gave no sign that he did and just went on with his clipping.

Mrs. Schroeder said to Mr. Schroeder, "The trouble with your mother is that even when she does something nice every once in

57

a blue moon, she's so disagreeable about it that it's hard to feel grateful."

"But she did do something nice, and that's what matters," Mr. Schroeder said. "When I phoned Perky last night and told him I had the dough, he was tickled to death. So let's just pack up our troubles for once and have a whiz of a day." And that's just the kind of day they had.

The first thing they did was walk down to the garage to get the funnies, Teddy holding one of Mr. Schroeder's hands and Bean the other. Almost all the Sunday newspapers had them then—not just a comic strip or two in black and white tucked away on the same page as the horoscopes and the cross-word puzzle but a whole full-color section of funnies and nothing else. There were ones that were supposed to make you laugh like The Katzenjammer Kids and Mutt and Jeff and Popeye, and adventure ones like Dick Tracy and Buck Rogers and Little Orphan Annie. One of Bean's favorites was The Timid Soul, which was about a henpecked husband named Caspar Milquetoast, and Teddy liked Mandrake the Magician mostly because of all the magic in it. They sat out in the sun on the piazza steps while Mr. Schroeder read some of them out loud. He would move his finger from one balloon caption to the next to show which character was speaking each time. That's the way he'd done it before they knew how to read for themselves, and they liked him to go on doing it that way still.

All the time he was reading, in the background they could hear Mr. Mittendorf cutting his lawn with the kind of push mower they had before there were power ones. When he rolled it forward to do the cutting, it sounded rattly and full of energy, but when he pulled it backward, it made a smoother, higher-pitched sound as if it was getting a little hysterical. The ducks were making sounds too. The children had scattered some popcorn left over from the birthday party down by the dock, and some of the ducks had waddled up on the bank to peck at it. When they weren't pecking, they would rise up on their yellow feet and flap their wings in the air.

Mrs. Schroeder had had breakfast in bed the way she usually did on Sundays—Mrs. Lundbeck would make her poached eggs on toast, which was her favorite, and Mr. Schroeder would carry her tray up to her—and they could hear her trying to sing "Me and My Shadow" as she was getting dressed.

She was so bad at carrying a tune that everybody said the only way you could tell what song it was supposed to be was to listen to the words. But it was nice to hear her singing anyway in a voice that was much deeper than her ordinary voice and sounded more like somebody groaning.

In fact all the sounds were nice, Teddy thought, and so was everything else. His mother and father, he and Bean, the ducks, Mr. Mittendorf—at least for the time being everybody was in the right place doing the right thing, and it gave him a very good feeling.

That afternoon they went to the beach. It was a Sunday, and the weather was so good that almost everybody was there, including even Grandma and Grandpa Schroeder. The sand was dotted with umbrellas and sunbathers. The men's bathing suits had tops to them then that looked like striped undershirts, and the ladies' had skirts that came down about to their knees. Lots of the ladies also wore rubber bathing shoes that buckled over the instep and protected their feet from pebbles. Some people were swimming out in the deep water, and you could see their heads bobbing about in the blue swells. Others were riding the waves, and Mr. Schroeder asked Teddy if he thought he would like to try riding a couple himself. They looked like pretty big ones as he watched them come rolling up on the sand, but he figured that as long as his father was with him everything would probably be all right, so he said he would. Bean and his mother sat under their umbrella and watched.

There were quite a few swimmers out there doing it, and Mr. Schroeder and Teddy joined them. They all stood in a line with their backs to the waves looking over their shoulders and waiting till one came along that seemed to be a good size. They were about up to Teddy's chest in the water. Mr. Schroeder said that the most important part of riding a wave was to catch it at just the right moment.

"If you catch it before it starts to break," he said, "it slips out from under you and leaves you behind looking silly. And if you catch it after it starts, you get rolled. The right time is just when it's about to curl over. As soon as that moment comes, start swimming as fast as you can to keep on top of the curl, and the next thing you know—whoopee—you're off. Stick with me, kiddo, and you'll see."

They let several waves go by—a couple

because they weren't big enough and one because it was too big. "A buster," Mr. Schroeder called it as he and Teddy jumped to keep their heads above water while it swept past them and went thundering toward the beach. Then they saw one coming that looked about right.

Mr. Schroeder said, "OK. Get ready—just a second—I'll tell you when." But before he had a chance to tell him, Teddy was off.

The trouble was that he was off too soon. Instead of being on top of the wave as it curled over, he was in the trough just in front of it, and before he could do anything about it, the whole mountain of water came crashing down on him and dragged him under. It tumbled him head over heels. It spun him around. It got up his nose and into his ears and pounded him against the sandy bottom. Everything was dark and crazy when suddenly he felt somebody grab him and in seconds he was in daylight again with his father holding him under the arms.

"If ever that happens again, I'll tell you what to do," his father said. "Don't fight it. It's much too big to fight. Just let it do what it wants with you. A few seconds and it's all over. It's even sort of fun being rolled if you just give in to it and don't hit back."

"I think you're crazy," Teddy said, but there was something about his father's face with his hair dripping like seaweed and his blue eyes a little bloodshot from the salt water and his flashing wet grin that made Teddy decide that maybe what he was saying was true.

After a while he caught another wave too soon and again he was rolled, but this time he did what his father had said. He just made himself limp and let the churning water play with him like a huge shaggy blue dog and in no time at all it had washed him up almost to the beach and left him none the worse for wear in the foaming shallows. He wouldn't have said it was fun exactly, but it wasn't all that bad either.

"And after all," his father said, "the wave is just trying to take you where you want to go anyway."

"Where do you mean?" Teddy asked.

"Why, the dry land. That's where waves go," his father said. "Home. Where else?" They both laughed.

He caught a couple of waves the right way too, and he and his father went shooting along on the backs of them with their arms stretched out straight over their heads. He liked it better than being rolled.

Mrs. Schroeder made him come out after a while. She said his lips were blue and he was shivering. So he and Bean played in the sun for a while. Bean got him to bury her in the sand with just her head sticking out and then had him add two more sand arms and two more sand legs to her so that she ended up looking like some kind of a human tarantula. When Mr. Schroeder leaned over to get a better look at her, two streams of salt water came running out of his nose, which Mrs. Schroeder said was revolting but which Bean thought was perfectly marvelous.

Grandpa Schroeder came over after a while on his gimpy leg. He had part of the Sunday papers with him, which he spread out on the sand as he sat down. He was wearing a pair of old dark blue bathing trunks with a couple of moth holes in them and a white canvas belt that had rust stains on it and a belt buckle that was two snakes looped around each other. Bean looked at his bare feet and said his big toenail looked like an apricot pit. The children couldn't remember ever having seen him laugh before. He didn't make much noise doing it, but it made him shake all over, and tears rolled down out of his watery eyes, dampening the corners of his drooping moustache.

But the best thing that happened that day was the second time Teddy and his father went swimming. Usually Bean was the one that Mr. Schroeder did things with whereas Teddy was more apt to get taken places by his mother, like downtown to go shopping or off somewhere to see one of her friends or to New York the way they did on his birthday. But this time it was the other way round.

Mrs. Schroeder had never learned to swim because she was afraid of the water and couldn't bear to get her face wet and also because she didn't want to ruin her permanent wave. She wore a bathing cap like all the other ladies, but she was afraid water would get in under it somehow. So what she did instead of swimming was pretend to swim. She would go in only about as deep as her waist, squat down so just her head and shoulders were showing above the surface, and then sweep her arms back and forth as if she was doing the breast stroke. Bean thought this was very funny and when Mrs. Schroeder did it this time, Bean went and squatted down in the water near her mother and did the same thing she was doing with her arms but also stretched one leg out as far behind her as she could reach so she could kick the water with her foot. She thought this made the whole thing look even more realistic.

Mr. Schroeder told Teddy that now he had learned how to ride waves, he was ready to swim out to the barrels. The barrels were quite a way from shore and had been anchored there to show that it wasn't safe to swim any farther. Only the stronger, more experienced swimmers went that far usually, and there were ropes tied between the barrels so there would be something for them to hang on to when they did. Mr. Schroeder said that he and Teddy would just take it easy and everything would be fine.

About half way there they came upon Grandma Schroeder swimming a little distance away. She was so fat that you might have thought she couldn't swim at all but you would have been wrong. She was so fat that she floated like a cork, and Mrs. Schroeder said it would take a torpedo to sink her. There she was bobbing around in the ocean with her white bathing cap strapped under her chin and her cheeks bulging out of it. She could hardly believe her eyes when she saw Teddy dog-paddling along beside his father. She waved at him and he waved back at her, and he was proud that she had seen him out so far and doing the kind of thing that she thought boys were supposed to do for a change.

She didn't look to him as if she could ever be cross. She didn't look as if she would ever say a mean thing to Grandpa about drinking too many highballs or about how if it wasn't for her father they'd all be in the poor house. She didn't look rich or fierce. She just looked as if she was having a good time. She looked jolly and friendly and almost young with her bathing cap bouncing up and down in the sun like a balloon.

But the best part of the day happened just a little while afterward. Teddy thought the barrels still looked a long way off, and the beach was so far behind he could hardly recognize his mother and Bean sitting on it. His arms were beginning to ache, and he was feeling out of breath. What if he started to drown, he thought? What if he called for help and his father, who was a little ahead of him, didn't hear? What if a giant octopus swam up from below and wrapped him in its slimy green tentacles?

But just as he was thinking these things,

his father turned around and treaded water, waiting for him.

"How about a lift the rest of the way?" Mr. Schroeder said. So Teddy paddled over and put his arms around his father's neck from behind, and that was the best part of the day for him and the part he remembered for many years afterward.

He remembered how the sunlight flashed off his father's freckly, wet shoulders and the feel of the muscles working inside them as he swam. He remembered the back of his father's head and the way his ears looked from behind and the way his hair stuck out over them. He remembered how his father's hair felt thick and wiry like a horse's mane against his cheek and how he tried not to hold on to his neck too tightly for fear he'd choke him.

His mother said bad things about his father. She said that he had no get-up-and-go and that he was worse than Grandpa Schroeder already though thirty years younger. She said he needed a swift kick in the pants and things like that. And Teddy knew that his father did things that he wished he wouldn't, like drink too many cocktails and drive his car up on the lawn and come to kiss him and

Bean goodnight with his face all clammy and cold.

But as he swam out toward the barrels on his father's back, he also knew that there was no place in the whole Atlantic ocean where he felt so safe.

six

A few days later it rained, and that was the kind of day that Teddy liked better than all other kinds. He loved to hear rain pattering on the roof and blowing against the window panes. He loved the smell of raincoats and rubber rainhats and the flip-flop, flip-flop of windshield wipers and the sizzling sound of tires on a wet road. He liked to walk in the rain with a red plaid umbrella that somebody had given him once, and he liked sitting outside in it in one of the deck chairs that had a canvas top that you could use to keep the sun off you. He would pull the top down and put an old tarpaulin he'd found in the garage over it and then sit there as if he was sitting in a tent and just watch the rain and listen to the rain and smell the smells things have when it's raining on them—things like the grass and the trees and the tarpaulin and his blue sweater.

What he liked most about it, though, was that it not only gave you a good excuse for

70

staying inside at home all day if you felt like it but that it made home seem homier and cozier than it did any other time. He also found out that any book you read when it's raining is at least twice as good as it is when it's not raining, and on this particular day he read two of them from start to finish. They were called Big Little books, chunky, square books about half the size of a brick that you could buy at Woolworth's for a dime. One of them was *Buck Rogers and the Planetoid Plot* and the other was *Tarzan Escapes*, which had pictures of Johnny Weissmuller and Maureen O'Sullivan in it.

It was getting on toward supper time when he finished the Tarzan one. He could smell whatever Mrs. Lundbeck was cooking in the kitchen downstairs. Bean was sitting at the bridge table drawing pictures and listening to Uncle Don on her white Mickey Mouse radio. Uncle Don began every show with the same song, which started out with the words, "Hello nephews, nieces, mine. I'm glad to see you look so fine" and ended "Horney-ka-dote with an alikazon, sing this song with your Uncle Don," which Bean hated so much that she always clapped her hands over her ears when it came to that part.

Then Teddy heard the sound of a car door

slam in the driveway and a pair of feet walking up the wooden back steps, and he knew that his father was home from the city.

Teddy had a way of hearing such things even when he wasn't especially listening for them. Just from the sounds he usually knew what room everybody was in and what they were doing there—Mrs. Lundbeck using the sewing machine in her stuffy bedroom on the third floor, for instance, or Mrs. Schroeder in the living room ringing up a friend on the telephone. If people were talking somewhere in the house, even if he couldn't hear the words they were saying, he could tell a lot just from the sounds their voices made. He could tell if they were cheerful. He could tell if they were mad. It was as if he felt he had to keep track of everything that was going on in the house pretty much all the time so in case anything went wrong he would be prepared for it even if there was nothing he could do about it.

Uncle Don was talking about how everybody should be an Earnest Saver and send in to him for a tin bank they could put their money in. Mrs. Lundbeck was in the kitchen using an eggbeater. The tree outside his window was blowing in the rain.

Then he heard his father walk into the

living room to tell Mrs. Schroeder he was home. It was his regular voice, low-pitched and quiet. He listened for his mother to answer, but he couldn't hear anything. Then his father spoke again. Then there was a loud bang as if somebody had thrown a book down on a table or slammed down a telephone receiver. Only then did he hear his mother's voice, and the sound of it made his blood run cold.

It wasn't her loud mad voice. It was her quiet mad voice. That meant she was much madder. He couldn't hear what she was saying, but he knew she was telling his father why she was mad. He looked to see if Bean was listening too, but she was too busy listening to her radio.

When his mother was through, he heard his father speak again, only in a different voice this time. This time it was his begging voice. Whatever he was begging her to do or not to do, though, he didn't have time to finish before Teddy heard a chair scrape back and the sound of his mother's high heels on the floor. Clickety-click out into the hall they went, with the living room door banging shut behind her. Then he didn't just hear his father run after her but felt the whole house shake under the weight of his footsteps. They were both in the front hall now. There was no way not to hear what they were saying. Even Bean now had to listen.

"You had absolutely no right to do it. You know that as well as I do," Mrs. Schroeder said. "I could have you put in jail. Those were my stocks, not yours. My father gave them to *me*. I can't believe you would pull such a dirty, rotten trick."

"But darling, I only did it for you and the kids," Mr. Schroeder said. "We've got to have just a little more cash so we can turn out a couple of samples of the glass. Then the money's going to start rolling in, I promise you. You'll have more stocks than you know what to do with. Perky says . . ."

"You and your beloved Perky," Mrs. Schroeder said. "If you ask me he's just playing you for a fool. He's just using you for what he can get out of you. You're so weak it makes me sick. Just look at you!"

"Darling, darling. Won't you listen to me?"

"We live in this awful house practically next door to a gas station. My clothes are so old I'm ashamed to be seen in them. We can't even afford piano lessons for the children. Never in my wildest dreams as a girl did I think it would come to this. Well, I'm through. I'm taking the children and getting out."

That was not all she said or maybe even the worst she said, but it was what Teddy remembered afterward when he thought about it, that and the way almost all his father had said back was things like "Please" and "Darling" in his begging voice. He remembered his father's silence too while she was saying those terrible things to him.

And all the time it was happening, Teddy was thinking about the magic word PYRZQXGL—not saying it because he didn't know how to say it but seeing it in his mind the way it looked on the Oz book page, that weird combination of letters, and thinking if only he could get it right somehow, he could make the awful fighting stop.

The way it did stop finally was that his mother came running up the stairs and right into the room where he and Bean were and shut the door so hard that it made the window rattle and turned the key in the lock. In a second or two Mr. Schroeder came up after her and tried to get her to let him in, but she wouldn't.

Nobody said anything for a few minutes,

and Mrs. Schroeder's face looked too terrible to look at.

Then out in the hallway Mr. Schroeder said, "I'm going to go over and see Father then," and Mrs. Schroeder said, "Yes, I bet you are. That's typical. *Typical*. You're two of a kind. You can get drunk together and tell him how you stole from your own wife."

They could all hear Mr. Schroeder go downstairs and leave the house then.

"Mommy, are you really going to go away and take us with you?" Teddy asked.

She was still standing at the locked door listening to make sure he was gone. Bean looked as white as her Mickey Mouse radio. Her topknot was shaking.

"I don't know what I'm going to do," Mrs. Schroeder said. "I honestly don't know."

She went into her own room then and was about to shut the door when she called back to them.

"Tell Mrs. Lundbeck just to feed you two in the kitchen," she said. "God knows when your father will be back, and after what I've been through, just the thought of food makes me feel sick."

In a queer way that was one of the worst parts of it all for Teddy and Bean. No matter what bad things happened, there had always been a few everyday things that kept going on the same as usual and helped them believe that someday everything would be all right again. One of them was meals. Unless Mr. and Mrs. Schroeder went out, the four of them almost always had supper together— Mr. Schroeder at one end of the dining room table and Mrs. Schroeder at the other and the children next to each other on the same side because they both liked to look out at the ducks on the canal. But now their father had gone away, and their mother was shut up in her room upstairs, and there were only the two of them left to have supper with Mrs. Lundbeck in the kitchen.

Mrs. Lundbeck must have heard every-thing just the way Teddy and Bean had, but she didn't say anything about it. They didn't say anything about it either, not even to each other. Mrs. Lundbeck tried to think of ways to cheer them up. She went all the way up to the third floor to get a pack of picture post-cards she'd saved from a trip she once took to Mexico and spread them out on the li-noleum so they could look at them while they were eating their corned beef hash. She said that on her next day off she would take them to a carnival she'd heard about in a town nearby where for twenty-five cents they showed you a boy who was covered with green scales and was half crocodile. Teddy found it hard to pay attention to what she was saying because he was listening so hard for the sound of his father coming back or of his mother coming out of her room.

What would happen if his father never came back, Teddy thought? What was his mother doing up there in her room? Maybe she was getting ready to take them all away.

Bean cheered up a little at the thought of seeing the crocodile boy, but when Mrs. Lundbeck suggested they could sing one of their goodnight songs right there in the kitchen, Bean didn't feel like it and neither did Teddy.

When it got to be their bedtime and Mr. Schroeder still hadn't come back, Mrs. Schroeder came out of her room and said that she didn't want to be alone. She asked Teddy to come sleep in his father's bed next to hers. Sleeping in his own bed was another of the everyday things that Teddy counted on to make him feel better, but he couldn't say no to her, so after he'd put on his pajamas and brushed his teeth, he went into her room and climbed in between his father's sheets. At least that way, he thought, he would know if she decided to pack her bags and leave.

He wanted to ask her what his father had stolen from her, but he didn't want to get her mad again so he just lay there not saying anything while she finished smoking a cigarette at the dressing table where she put her makeup on in the mornings.

She was just about to put out the light and go say goodnight to Bean when he heard the front door open and somebody come in. In a moment he heard his father calling up the stairs.

"Connie," he said. "Come down, Connie. I've got to ask you something."

Teddy didn't know whether his father was drunk or not, but he thought his voice sounded funny.

"Oh God," his mother said and went downstairs.

They must have shut the door when they went into the living room because Teddy couldn't hear anything they were saying. But at least it didn't sound mad this time. Once he even thought he heard his father laughing. Just before he'd heard the clattery sound of something dropping to the floor, and he thought maybe his father was laughing at that. Then the door must have opened again because now he heard his mother clearly.

"Please just stay there, Ted," she said. "I'll be back in a second."

Before he knew it, she was standing beside his bed. She must have tiptoed up the stairs.

"These are the keys to the car," she said. "I want you to keep them." She handed him the keys. "Your father's in no shape to drive and you're not to give them to him no matter what. Do you understand what I'm saying?"

"Why can't he drive the Pierce Arrow?" Teddy asked.

"It's broken," she said. "The Pierce Arrow is at the garage, and it's broken."

After a while Mr. Schroeder came up.

Teddy didn't know how his father knew he had the keys. Maybe his mother had told him. Maybe he guessed. His mother was over by the window now. His father was standing by the bed staring down at him. He looked pale and sweaty. He had on his gabardine suit still, but he'd undone his collar button and pulled down his necktie half way. Teddy could tell by the way he was looking at him that he knew he had the keys. Teddy had them clenched in his fist and his fist was under the pillow.

"Please can I have the keys to the car, Teddy?" he said.

Teddy didn't know what to say so he said nothing at all. He didn't want to look at his father.

"I need them right now, Teddy," his father said. "I've got to drive someplace. Please let me have them."

"I should think you'd be ashamed," his mother said from where she was standing by the window. "I should think you'd be ashamed to let your own son see you like this."

Mr. Schroeder turned for a moment as if to say something to her but then sat down on the other twin bed. After a while, he held out his hand toward Teddy. It was close enough for Teddy to touch, but he didn't touch it.

"Please, Teddy," his father said. "I'm begging you to give them to me."

Teddy pulled the covers over his head because he didn't know what else to do. He tightened his fist on the keys till they dug into his fingers. He wondered if his father would rip the covers off him and grab them out of his hand. He hoped he would because then at least it would all be over.

"Please," he could hear his father saying.

He said it many more times before he finally left, just that one word over and over again. Sometimes there was such a long pause in between that Teddy would think he'd gone, but he was too scared to peek out from under the covers to see.

He thought of the word PYRZQXGL again. He tried to think of any word among all the words in the world that he could say out loud now for his mother and father both to hear which would change everything into being all right. Then he would be back in his own bed where he belonged, and his father would be in his and his mother in hers. The rain would be pattering against the window pane, and he would say, "Are you asleep, Bean?" and she would say, "No, Are you?" And then they would decide where to go when they were asleep and they would go there.

"Please, Teddy," Mr. Schroeder said, but Teddy didn't hear him.

It was very hot and stuffy there with the covers over his head. He hadn't thought he was at all drowsy, but he had felt so tired his whole body ached, and before he even knew what he was doing—still holding the car keys tight in his fist—he had fallen fast asleep in his father's bed.

seven

One of the strangest things about the Schroeder family was that when bad things happened, nobody ever talked about them afterward. The day after the car keys business is an example.

Mr. Schroeder spent the night on the living room couch. Teddy heard him coming up the stairs to take his shower and shave the next morning, and while he was still in the bathroom, Teddy got up. First he laid the keys down on top of the pillow because he figured that it didn't matter any more whether his father took them or not. Then he tiptoed out of his parents' bedroom, where his mother was still asleep, and crawled back into his own bed next to Bean's.

When he saw his father at breakfast, his father didn't say anything about what had happened, and when he saw his mother, she didn't say anything either. Teddy himself didn't bring the subject up, of course. He was afraid that if he did, they might start fighting all over again or maybe start fighting at him. When he saw his father and mother together later that day, they didn't even talk about it to each other. They were both more silent than usual and you could tell from their faces and the way they didn't look at each other very much that something was wrong, but that was as far as it went. If he hadn't known better, he would have thought that the whole thing had been just a bad dream. That's what everybody pretended, including Teddy and Bean when they were alone in their room together. They didn't talk about it either.

Teddy could even pretend to *himself* that it had never happened. The Oz books and going to the beach and things like that helped. They made it easier for him to forget how fights scared him so much that they made his scalp feel cold as ice. But the scared feeling itself was still there inside him even so. He couldn't forget that.

He didn't connect it with the fights any more, the way he connected being scared of fox terriers with a fox terrier named Trixie who bit him once when he reached out to pat her. And because he didn't connect the scared feeling with what really scared him, it was free to connect itself with anything it felt like. That's why all sorts of things scared him that didn't bother other people at all, not even Bean.

What he was *really* scared of was that someday his mother and father would have such an awful fight that one of them, or maybe even both of them, would leave forever and Bean and he wouldn't have any place to go. But he pretended like the rest of the family that there never were any such fights, and so what scared him instead were little things.

If his mother left the house without telling him where she was going, or if his father was late coming back from New York the way he had been on his birthday, it scared him. If he was upstairs in his room and suddenly realized that there wasn't a sound anywhere in the whole house, it scared him. Little things like that.

But then one day not long before it was time to leave the house by the canal and go back to New Jersey again, something happened that made all those things fade away like dark corners in a room when you turn on the lights. What happened was that the children's other grandmother came all the way from Pittsburgh by train to visit them.

Their name for her was Dan. Teddy was the one who started calling her that when he was very little, though why he did he couldn't have told you any more than he could have told you why he started calling Bean by the name of Bean instead of by her real name (which she hated), which was Ruth. Dan was the one who lived in the big house with the sleeping porch and the billiard room with the moose head in it.

She had gray hair, which she wore in a bun on the back of her head, and if Teddy and Bean happened to be around in the morning when she was getting up, she would let them come in and watch her fix it. She would stand in front of the mirror in her nightdress and first plait it into a long braid that hung down almost as far as her waist. Then she would coil it around and around on the back of her head till it was all used up and stick several big tortoise-shell hairpins in it to hold it in place. The hairpins held it in place very well, but toward the end of the day there would usually be a few stray wisps of hair floating in the air.

She was also very fond of knitting socks for people, and when she was turning the heel, which she said was by far the hardest part, she always said, "For pity's sake don't anybody talk to me *now*." When she knitted, she wore the kind of glasses that don't go over your ears the way most glasses do but the kind that just clip onto the bridge of your nose, which are called pince-nez. They hung around her neck on a black ribbon that had a little diamond clasp on it. When the children were quite a bit younger she told them the clasp was a peck bird who would tell them stories sometimes and sometimes just try to peck them.

Not many old ladies smoked cigarettes in those days, but Dan did. She smoked them in white paper cigarette holders, which she would throw away as soon as they showed signs of turning yellow. She loved doing the big crossword puzzle in the Sunday papers, finishing it before most people had done much more than get their pencils sharpened, and like Teddy she also loved reading books. Charles Dickens was one of her favorite writers, and she would talk to him about people like Mr. Micawber and Madame Defarge and Samuel Pickwick as if they were old friends. And she also told him about all sorts of real people too. They were mostly aunts and cousins and great-grandparents and so on whom he had never seen, but she was so good at describing the odd things they'd done and the queer old citizens they'd been that he got to feel that he'd known them as well as she had and could sit hours at a time while she went on about them. Dan loved to talk and Teddy loved to listen, and that was why they always seemed to enjoy being with each other almost more than they enjoyed being with anybody else.

One day during the week she stayed with the Schroeders, and everybody had something to do except for the two of them. Bean's friend Sally Hartman had asked her over for the night, and Mr. and Mrs. Schroeder were going to a dance at a nightclub called Canoe Place out toward Montauk Point, and Dan said that it seemed a shame to keep Mrs. Lundbeck in to cook supper just for Teddy and her.

"Since the whole crowd seems to be deserting us, let's you and me make a night of it," Dan said. "We will put on our gladdest rags and get somebody for a price to drive us down to the Sagapac House, and we will launch ourselves into high society. First we will sit out on the veranda in a pair of those venerable green rockers and watch the world go by, and then we will hie us to the dining room and have the kind of feast of which legends are made. No expense is to be spared. We will order the shrimp cocktail to start with if it strikes our fancy or maybe six lovely fresh oysters on the half shell, and we will end up with a dessert of unspeakable decadence. Then if there is a good movie in town, we may decide to take that in too. Who knows what adventures we will have before we're through. What do you say to all that, my dear boy?"

"Let's ditch Canoe Place and go with them," Mr. Schroeder said, and Mrs. Schroeder said, "Two's company, four's a crowd."

The Schroeders were all dressed up to make an early start for Canoe Place because they had to pick up friends on the way, Mr. Schroeder in his tuxedo and shiny black shoes and Mrs. Schroeder in the same pink evening dress that Grandma Schroeder had told her she must think she was married to a millionaire to be able to afford. They both looked very nice, Teddy thought, and they didn't just *look* nice either. They said nice things to each other. Mrs. Schroeder told Dan that Mr. Schroeder was such a divine dancer that all the ladies wanted him to cut in on them, and Mr. Schroeder said that as far as he was concerned there was only one lady he was interested in dancing with, and he guessed everybody knew who *that* was. And other things like that.

People were almost always nice to each other when Dan was around. It wasn't because they were afraid of her the way they were afraid of Grandma Schroeder but because she always looked so peaceful and contented as she sat in her chair taking an occasional puff on her cigarette or knitting a sock that it made people feel peaceful and contented themselves just to be in the same room with her. It's when you're feeling like that, of course, that you're apt to be nicest.

The taxi man drove them right up to the main entrance of the Sagapac House where there were several bellboys in white trousers with stripes down the sides and green blazers waiting to carry people's bags up to their rooms for them if they were planning on spending the night. It was a very large three-story white frame building with a broad lawn in front that had both a croquet court and a putting green on it. There was also a veranda on the ocean side that ran from one end of the building to the other, and lots of people were sitting out there when Teddy and his grandmother arrived.

The ladies all had pretty, short-sleeved dresses on and smelled of perfume when you passed behind their chairs, and the men wore things like white ducks, which is what they called white pants then, and saddle shoes, and jackets with belts at the back. They were all talking to each other and laughing and rattling the ice cubes in their glasses, and it made an exciting, cheerful sound a little bit like the clinking noise milk bottles used to make when the milkman drove his truck over a bump. You would never have known there was a Depression on to see them.

Suddenly Teddy noticed that his friend Virginia Miller was there too. He spotted her as the waiter led him and Dan to their rockers at the far end of the veranda, and it made his stomach feel tight inside. She still looked like Alice in Wonderland, with a ribbon tied around her long hair, and she waved at him over the shoulders of her parents as he passed by. Teddy gave her a small wave back again, but he was too shy to go over and say anything to her.

It was still a bright sunny day, but the sun was starting to get lower in the sky and the light had that golden look to it that it does toward the end of the afternoon. The breeze had died down, and the ocean was quite smooth except that every once in a while there would be a wave. You would see a slowly moving ridge of water quite a way out and you wouldn't think it was going to amount to much but then when it got in close to shore it would rear up and curl over and hit down on the beach with a slap. Then in a few moments there was the hissing sound it made when it drained back over the sand into the ocean again.

Dan ordered a glass of iced tea and Teddy ordered a ginger ale, which came with a straw and a corkscrew twist of lemon peel in it. Then Dan lit a Chesterfield, which was the brand she always used. She blew a puff of smoke into the air between them and narrowed her eyes at him through it in an intense and penetrating sort of way.

"That is my riverboat gambler look," she said. "And this is to your good health."

She lifted up her glass, and Teddy lifted up his, and they clinked the two of them together.

"In France they call that *le carillion d'amitié*," Dan said, "which means the ting-a-ling of friendship in case you would like to know."

Then she started talking the way she loved to, and Teddy sat there drinking his ginger ale and listening to her. She told him about how when she was about Bean's age, not long after George Washington chopped down the cherry tree she said, boys his age were always doing terrible things to girls. Once some of them told her to put her tongue on the icy cold runner of her sled, she said, and when she did, it got so stuck she couldn't get it off till her mother came out of the house and poured a cup of warm tea on it. Another time they told her if she would just eat a poison ivy sandwich, she would never get poison ivy, so she made herself one and ate it, and "As God is my witness," she said, "I have never gotten it to this day."

She also told him about her cousin Frank, who could make the hens lay when nothing else would work by going out into the hen coop and reciting the words to the Gettysburg Address to them in a certain way he knew. And about how when she was first grown up people still used ear trumpets and one evening Teddy's grandfather accidentally tipped his whole cup of after-dinner coffee into one that an old lady had stuck out toward him when she was trying to hear what he was saying to her.

After a while, she asked Teddy what he had been doing lately. She didn't ask it just to be polite the way grown-ups often do but because when she took a fancy to people, she liked listening to them almost as much as she liked talking. So Teddy told her. He told her how his father had been trying to teach him the proper way to ride waves, and he told her how he had been rolled by a couple of them and what it had felt like while it was going on.

"I can hardly think of anything under the sun I would less want to do myself even if I could swim, which I can't, just like your dear mother," Dan said. "I would pay cash money to get out of it."

"It's scary all right," Teddy said. "But Daddy says if you don't fight the waves they'll always bring you back to shore because that's where they're going too."

"Well, I suppose that's true," Dan said. "But it would be just like me to get caught in a sea puss instead, I'm afraid."

Teddy had rather big eyes, and sometimes they were apt to get even bigger.

"What's that?" he said.

"Why it's the undertow, my poor ignorant boy," she said. "The waves bring you in all right if you know what you're doing, but there's always a sea puss somewhere just licking its chops for a chance to drag some respectable matron who doesn't know how to swim the other way."

"There are a lot more waves than there are sea pusses though," Teddy said, "and they're much stronger."

"Of course they are," she said. "And what's more, the sea pusses always give up after a while but the waves never do."

Dan had let the ash on her cigarette grow so long that when she moved her hand, it fell off onto the arm of her green rocker.

"It is also a rule of life that no matter how far the low tide goes out," she said, "the high tide always comes in again as high as ever. I suppose that's a handy thing to remember when you're feeling a little low yourself."

"Do you feel low ever, Dan?" Teddy asked.

"Sometimes I feel like going out in the garden and chewing worms," she said.

"I wish bad things didn't happen," Teddy said.

"It would be nice, there's no question about that," Dan said. "But the way things are, I guess all you can do is wait for them to unhappen. In the long run they usually seem to."

"I guess so," Teddy said.

"And in the meanwhile, make yourself scarce if you see a sea puss heading in your direction," she said. "And try to catch the tide at the flow."

"The one that brings you in," Teddy said.

"The very one," Dan said, "and if you keep making that appalling noise with your straw, my poor benighted child, the management will probably throw us out."

Neither of them ordered the shrimp cocktail when the time came. Teddy had a cup of cold white potato soup with little snippets of green chive in it, which Dan told him you were supposed to order in fancy places like the Sagapac House even if you didn't feel like it, and they were both pleasantly surprised when Teddy liked it. Dan had oysters on the half shell, which she said were supposed to be so fresh that you could see them wince when you squeezed lemon on them but she didn't want to think about it. After that they both had lamb chops with frilly paper cuffs on them and rather sticky rice and broccoli with hollandaise sauce, which wasn't curdled the way the kind Mrs. Lundbeck made usually was.

The dining room was full of people talking and eating and smoking cigarettes, and every table had a skinny vase with two or three red roses in it. One whole wall was nothing but windows, and you could see the sun setting through it—a stripe of yellow and a stripe of pink and then a sort of pale greenish blue down toward where the sky and the water met. There was a woman in a long dress playing the piano and a man in a white jacket with a rose in his buttonhole playing the violin, but you could hardly hear them over the sound of everything else.

It was while they were waiting for the waiter to bring them dessert—Teddy got strawberry shortcake and his grandmother a small dish of orange ice with a mint leaf stuck in it—that Teddy felt somebody tap him on his shoulder from behind. When he turned around, he found it was Virginia Miller.

"I got two of these from Mother and Dad's rum swizzles," she said, "and this one is for you."

It was a swizzle stick with the name Sagapac House printed on it in green letters, and when Virginia Miller leaned over to hand it to him, the smell of her hair was so sweet and it felt so soft when it brushed against his cheek that it made him feel a little dizzy.

"There's a wonderful movie in town, Ted," she said. "You ought to see it if you haven't already," and then before he had time to do more than mutter thank you, she was off in a cloud of Conti Castille shampoo.

They found out at the desk that the movie was one called *Green Pastures*, and they decided to go. It was about God and the Bible, and all the actors and actresses in it were black people, though in those days they were called colored people or Negroes, instead. God was an old black preacher with a deep voice and a beard whom everybody called De Lawd, and every once in a while the archangel Gabriel would offer him a five cent seegar. Heaven was a big fish fry where all the angels and cherubs flew around with wings sticking out of their backs, eating their fried fish with corn bread and boiled custard to go with it. Adam and Eve were in it, Adam in overalls and Eve in a gingham dress, and so were Noah and Moses.

One of Teddy's favorite parts was where Moses forced the wicked old Pharaoh to let the Hebrew slaves go by showing him a lot of magic tricks, one of which was to throw his rod on the ground where it turned into a real snake right before your eyes. He also liked the part in De Lawd's office where De Lawd tells Gabriel there are a few things he wants him to attend to while he is away— one of them is "dat matter of dem two stars,"

De Lawd says, and the other "dat sparrow dat fell a little while ago."

"Do you think God is really like that?" Teddy asked while they were outside waiting for the taxi to come pick them up afterward.

None of the Schroeders went to church, neither Teddy's parents nor his grandparents. Grandma Schroeder said that she didn't believe in it, and Mrs. Schroeder said it always made her cry. The two men Schroeders never said why they didn't go—they just didn't. So Teddy and Bean didn't go to church either and didn't know anything much about what went on in it except for that one hymn, "The Old Rugged Cross," which they sang with Mrs. Lundbeck in the dark when she put them to bed.

"I hope he is like that," Dan said. She didn't go to church much either because she said it made her stomach rumble so loudly that it was embarrassing. "I hope he is as good and kind as that old colored man. And most of all I hope he is very powerful. He's going to need every bit of power he has to do all the things that need to be done in this poor old world."

"Power?" Teddy said.

"Power like the waves, Teddy," she said.

"I mean power enough to bring old sinners like me home."

When they got back, the house was dark as pitch because Mrs. Lundbeck had gone to bed and Bean was at the Hartmans and Mr. and Mrs. Schroeder probably wouldn't return from their dance till almost morning.

"I miss having young people around the way I used to when your mother was little," Dan said when they got upstairs. "It's very dull having nobody much to take care of any more except myself."

"Do you take care of yourself?" Teddy asked.

"Of course I do," she said. "I try to do a nice thing for myself every day or so if I can get around to it."

"Such as?"

A lot of wisps were floating out of Dan's bun by now, and she brushed a few of them back with her hand.

"Such as going off with you to supper and the movies all in one memorable night," she said.

"I thought you were doing that for me," Teddy said.

"Now and then it's possible to do a nice thing for two," she said as she put her hand

on the doorknob to open the guest room
door. "Those are generally the nicest ones
of all."

eight

All summer long people were talking about the king of England and Mrs. Simpson. Mrs. Simpson was an American lady who was supposed to be in love with the king of England even though she was already married to Mr. Simpson. There were pictures of her in every newspaper and every magazine. She was skinny and had black hair. King Edward usually looked puzzled and sad as if he knew something unpleasant was about to happen to him. Not long after the Schroeders got back to New Jersey from Sagapac the big headlines were that Mr. and Mrs. Simpson had been divorced so now there was no reason why she and the king couldn't get married if that's what they wanted to do.

People didn't get divorced as much then as they do now, and when the parents of one of Teddy's fifth-grade classmates named Betsy Deever did it, it was as if somebody had died in her family and nobody was ever supposed to mention it in front of her. Teddy and Bean weren't even sure what the word *divorce* meant until their mother told them. Teddy wondered if Mr. and Mrs. Deever had had lots of fights before it happened and what would become of Betsy now that it had. He also wondered about the king and Mrs. Simpson. Was he going to marry her and make her the queen? Some people said the government wouldn't let him because she had been divorced, and if so, then what?

"One way or the other she'll get him to marry her," Mr. Schroeder said. "No woman wants to stay unmarried if she can help it."

"You really think so?" Mrs. Schroeder said. "Well, if I were you, I wouldn't bet my bottom dollar on it."

"If things don't start looking up soon," Mr. Schroeder said, "I won't have my bottom dollar left to bet."

Perky was supposed to be getting closer and closer to turning out some samples of the heat-proof glass that was going to make them all rich. Mr. Schroeder had had to borrow money on his life insurance so he could help pay for the laboratory and everything. He had first tried to borrow another thousand dollars from Grandma Schroeder, but she had turned him down flat.

"Say, you must think I'm as rich as John D. Rockefeller," she said. "I'm not. And even if I was, I would be smart enough not to throw good money after bad. My father always said that friendship and business don't mix. He didn't get where he did being a soft touch."

But Mr. Schroeder got the money from his life insurance finally, and he kept on saying that within a year they would all be sitting pretty. In the meantime, though, he kept on looking for a job.

Every morning he would walk instead of drive down to the station to save on gas money and catch the train into New York, and every evening he would come back with no good news to report. Sometimes Teddy and Bean would go pick him up with their mother, and they could tell by the way he came walking down the train platform toward them that he still hadn't found what he was after. Teddy remembered how brown and strong and jolly he'd been when they went swimming in the surf together, and it was hard to believe that the tired-looking man with the evening paper under his arm and the five o'clock shadow was even the same person. Sometimes he would be so tired that he would just have his cocktails and then go to bed without any supper. Those were the times Teddy dreaded most, because it was when his mother and father were having cocktails together that his mother was most apt to get mad. From his room upstairs he would hear them chattering away as if they didn't have a care in the world, and then suddenly, the next moment, he would hear everything change.

"Never in my wildest dreams as a girl did I think it would come to this" was how she often started off, and Teddy would wonder what those long-ago dreams had really been like and how much worse things were for her now.

There were other times, though, when they would invite friends over to play Monopoly with them after supper. Monopoly had just been invented then and everybody was playing it.

"It's great to have money in your hands again even if it's play money," Teddy heard his father say once, and he thought maybe that was why they all liked to play it so much. People landing on Boardwalk with a hotel on it and going bankrupt having to pay the rent. People being sent to jail. People making a fortune. Sometimes his father got to laughing so loud that he could hear him even from upstairs with the radio on. It was not at all like the way he had laughed at Sagapac, but Teddy thought it was nice to hear him doing it any way he could.

The house needed people laughing in it, he thought. It was dark inside most of the time because of the woods all around it, and the lady they rented it from, who was an artist, had done a big charcoal drawing on the staircase wall that he and Bean both thought was awful. It showed an almost life-sized man sitting on an almost life-sized horse and the man had some kind of long spear in his hand that seemed to point right at them whenever they were on their way upstairs to their room.

October went pretty much the way September had, and November started out about the same. Bean didn't like her third-grade teacher very much because she said she had bad breath when she leaned over your shoulder to look at your paper and because she was much nicer to the boys in her class than she was to the girls. She also told Bean that she should get rid of her topknot because she was too old for it and have her mother make her some sausage curls with a curling iron instead. All little girls were supposed to look like Shirley Temple in those days, but Bean wasn't the least interested. Teddy told her she looked enough like a sausage even without the curls, and though he said it only to be funny, she was so upset that she went and sat in the dark at the back of the cellar and wouldn't come up till Teddy went down and promised he'd give her the sword to his drum major costume if only she wouldn't make a fuss and get their mother mad at them.

"When you kids start fighting with each other, I really don't think I can stand it any longer," she would say, and it made Teddy feel the same way he did when she said something was the last straw. If she really decided she couldn't stand it any longer some day, *then* what would she do?

Teddy liked school better than Bean did because he could do the work better. The only thing he didn't like about it much was Mr. Schultz, the gym and manual training teacher. Mr. Schultz said he wanted all the boys to start learning how to box, and one day he paired them off and showed them how to keep their guard up with one glove and jab out at their opponent with the other. Teddy was paired off with a boy named Bert Goodman, who had a fat, brown face and kinky hair, and they were standing there jabbing at each other without getting much of anywhere when suddenly Teddy must have not held his guard up high enough because Bert Goodman gave him such a hard punch right square on his nose it made tears run down out of his eyes. The only reason the tears ran down out of his eyes was that that is what happens automatically when anybody's nose gets hit hard that way, but that was not how Mr. Schultz saw it.

"If you go on bawling like that, everybody's going to think you're a sissy, Schroeder," Mr. Schultz said. "You just give him back some of his own medicine now."

Teddy gave it a try. He poked out as hard as he could at Bert Goodman's fierce, fat face, but Bert Goodman jumped sideways just in time, and the next thing Teddy knew, Bert's glove had caught him in exactly the same place again. This time he could feel blood trickling down out of his nostrils and could taste it on the inside of his upper lip.

"Easy does it, Bert," Mr. Schultz said, but Teddy could see he was pleased by what had happened. "It'll make a man out of you instead of a mouse, Schroeder," he said, and Teddy thought if that's what being a man was all about, maybe being a mouse wouldn't seem so bad.

It wasn't until late in November that anything very exciting happened, and then two exciting things happened one right on top of the other. The first of them was that on Thanksgiving Day there was a big snow. Grandpa and Grandma Schroeder had been driven out by Paul, their chauffeur, the evening before so they would be there for Thanksgiving dinner, and when Bean and Teddy woke up the next morning, the ground was already white with it, and it was still coming down in those small, steady flakes that usually mean it's going to keep snowing all day. Before Mrs. Lundbeck had even started getting breakfast ready, they put on their galoshes and mittens and winter coats and went out into it.

"It's so *quiet*, Teddy," Bean said. She stood on the front lawn with her wool hat pulled down over her eyebrows and stuck her tongue out as far as it would go so that some of the flakes would land on it. Other flakes had already gathered in her eyelashes. She was right, of course. Snow probably doesn't make things any quieter than usual *really*, but it always seems to. For one thing it falls more quietly than anything else in the world, and, for another, if you listen as hard as you can, you can sometimes hear just the faintest, farthest away, most delicate kind of whispery sound happening at the same time. It's as if it's the quiet itself that is whispering, and that makes it seem even quieter still.

It wasn't deep enough yet to make a snowman with or go sliding on, so the children just walked around and looked at it and listened to it and smelled it. Bean thought it had a smell anyway. She thought it was like the damp smell a pillowcase has if you happen to spill a little out of your water glass on it at night when you're taking a drink. The roof of Mr. Schroeder's Pierce Arrow was covered with it like icing on a birthday cake and so were the branches of the pine trees. They walked around to the kitchen windows to see if Mrs. Lundbeck had breakfast ready yet, and there were little dabs of snow in the corners of each of the square panes just like a Christmas card. Mrs. Lundbeck was trying to get the turkey and the creamed onions and the squash and everything else ready in addition to breakfast, so the kitchen was full of steam. The children flattened their noses and mouths against the glass so that from the inside they would look like monsters, and when Mrs. Lundbeck noticed them, she stopped dead in her tracks and just for a split second popped her teeth at them.

The second exciting thing happened during Thanksgiving dinner itself. They didn't sit down until almost three o'clock in the afternoon because they had lots of cocktails first, which Grandpa Schroeder made, holding the shaker up to his ear as he shook it so he'd know when they were ready to pour. The white table cloth was set with all the best silver and glassware and monogrammed napkins, and there were little paper baskets of chocolate pennies at every place. In the center was a big bowl full of oranges and grapes and kumquats and dried raisins and different kinds of queer-looking nuts some of which had shells too hard to crack. On the sideboard were laid out the two pies that Anna had sent out from the city, one of them mince and the other pumpkin. Mr. Schroeder sat at the head of the table and Mrs. Schroeder sat at the foot, with Grandpa Schroeder and Bean on one side facing Grandma Schroeder and Teddy on the other.

Grandpa Schroeder, who usually didn't talk very much, told a very long story about something that happened to him on the golf course once, but he told it in such a mumbly, rambling sort of way that nobody was quite sure what it was all about, and Grandma Schroeder got to squealing with laughter so hard that she had to hold her napkin up in front of her face. There was a bottle of red wine at one end of the table and a bottle of white wine at the other, and when they all had the kind they wanted, Mr. Schroeder stood up in front of his chair and said he had a few things he wanted to say.

He started out saying how glad he was his parents had come out from the city to be with them, and how even though times were bad they all had lots to be thankful for, and how well everybody was looking, and what a great story teller Grandpa Schroeder was, and some other things like that. His eyes sparkled and he laughed a lot and Teddy thought he looked more the way he had on the beach at Sagapac than he'd seen him for a long time. Then he said he had an announcement to make.

"Connie," he said, bowing in the direction of Mrs. Schroeder at the opposite end of the table, "this is especially for you to hear, darling. And Mother, you too—the two most important women in my life, except for this cuddly little lima Bean here. I know you've both had your doubts about things sometimes, but you've both come through with

112

help when I needed it most, and I plan to make it up to you very soon. In fact that's what my announcement is all about anyway so I guess I'll just come out with it without any more ado."

He stopped as if to catch his breath, and there were beads of perspiration on his forehead where his hair was beginning to recede a little.

"Upstairs in my closet right this minute there is a box, and in the box there are two bottles made of a new kind of glass that nothing will break come hell or hot water. If things work out the way Perky and I hope, we'll be going into production around about next summer and then the world will find out what this wonderful stuff really will do. But you lucky people won't have to wait as long as that because this very afternoon after Mrs. Lundbeck has finished doing the dishes—you kids will give her a hand, won't you?—I'm going to put on a demonstration in the kitchen that will have your eyes popping right out of your heads."

There were the same kind of oh's and ah's from all of them then that you hear from a Fourth of July crowd when the skyrockets start going off. Grandpa Schroeder didn't seem to understand at first what all the excitement was about, and Grandma Schroeder told him he'd better drink white wine the next time because he had gotten the red all over his moustache. Mrs. Schroeder came around behind her husband's chair to give him a hug and say how proud she was of him. And almost before Teddy and Bean had finished their dessert—they each had a piece of Anna's hot mince pie with a lump of hard sauce to melt on top—they were out in the kitchen helping Mrs. Lundbeck clean up.

All this time it had kept on snowing, and by the time the whole family including Mrs. Lundbeck was out in the kitchen ready to watch the demonstration, it was deep enough to have almost covered the bucket that Mr. Schroeder left out on the driveway the last time he and Bean had washed the good car. On the stove he had the big speckled blue pot they usually used for cooking corn-on-the-cob in full of water that was boiling so hard you could hear it bubbling.

The first thing he did was take out the watch that he wore only on special occasions. It was a gold pocket watch on a gold chain that Grandma and Grandpa Schroeder had given him when he graduated from college, and on the back it had his initials T. S. engraved on it in fancy letters with lots of curlicues on them. He often told Teddy, who had exactly the same initials, that someday it would belong to him.

He handed the watch to Teddy now and said that he was to be the timer. After he put the bottles in the water, Teddy was to say when five minutes were up because that should be long enough to convince anybody. The bottles were about the same shape as milk bottles only a little smaller, and Mr. Schroeder put them in very carefully, one by one.

The first one filled up and sank to the bottom right away. The second one floated on top and bobbed about, rattling against the sides of the blue pot. Teddy stayed over by the window so he could keep his eye on the time, but the rest of them all gathered around the stove watching. Grandpa Schroeder, who was a little unsteady on his feet, leaned up against the shelf where the spices were kept and knocked a box of pepper to the floor, but when Mrs. Lundbeck started to get a dustpan to sweep it up, Mr. Schroeder held out one arm to show her that nobody was to do anything or say anything till Teddy said it had been five minutes.

According to the gold watch, it had been exactly one minute and a half when the thing happened. There was such a loud pop that Mrs. Schroeder gave a little yelp and jumped back from the stove. Grandpa Schroeder also moved back and almost lost his balance stepping on the pepper box. Grandma Schroeder just stood there with her dinner napkin still tucked into the front of her dress shaking her head.

The floating bottle was the one that had popped. It had cracked apart lengthwise right down the middle. When Mr. Schroeder fished the other one out with a pair of tongs, it looked at first as if it was still all in one piece. It was only when he turned it over that they could see that the bottom had broken off as neatly as if somebody had cut it with a saw and was still sitting in the blue pot full of water boiling on the stove.

nine

The snow plow came the next morning while the children were getting dressed. They heard it rumbling and scraping in their driveway, and when they looked out the window, they could hardly believe their eyes. It must have gone on snowing well into the night. There were places where it had drifted as high as the bottom of the downstairs windows. A couple of lawn chairs that hadn't been put away yet were almost covered. While it was clearing the driveway so cars could get in and out, the plow had already made a huge pile almost as tall as the garage. There was no school that day because of the Thanksgiving holiday, and Teddy and Bean could hardly wait to get out in it. Other children were out already. They could see a few of them walking down the road in their red caps and mittens, dragging their sleds behind them.

They had slept later than usual because of all the excitement the day before, and when they got down, they found that Grandma and Grandpa Schroeder had already eaten and were standing at the living room window watching the plow at work. Their suitcases were out in the hall with their coats on top of them. They were supposed to go back to New York that morning, and Grandma Schroeder was very nervous about it because of the weather. She was nibbling at her fingernails and making small unpleasant remarks to Grandpa Schroeder as if it was mostly his fault. Grandpa Schroeder was smoking his pipe and staring out the window.

Grandma Schroeder turned when she heard Teddy and Bean come down the stairs, and they knew they ought to go in and be polite even though they were dying to have their breakfast and get outside as quickly as possible.

"Ted, won't you *please* call the police the way I asked and find out about the roads?" Grandma Schroeder said to her husband. "I'm so upset I don't know what to do, and you just stand there. I can't imagine where Paul is with the car."

Then she held out her arms toward the children and they went up and let her hug them. She always smelled a little bit of moth-balls.

"I feel so badly about your poor father," she said. "He is upstairs phoning that Perky man right now, though if you ask me he might just as well save his breath. When I think of the money he has poured into that idiotic business—money he had to beg, borrow, and steal because he certainly didn't have any of his own—it makes me so angry I don't know what to do. My father always said if you can't pay your own way, don't go, and he was right. You all of you live so extravagantly. You can't possibly afford Mrs. Lundbeck. She should be given her notice immediately. And your mother spends more on clothes in a month than I would think of spending in a year. There are certainly going to have to be some changes now, mark my word. You can't possibly go on living in this house. Your father will simply have to stop being so fussy about the kind of job he will take and do whatever comes along even if it's just pumping gas in a gas station. And you are going to have to help too, Teddy. You are nearly twelve years old. There is no reason on earth you couldn't bring some money in. You could find work delivering newspapers. Most boys your age are doing it these days. All you do is read a lot of silly books and let your mother drag you around on her apron strings. There is a terrible Depression going on, you know, and we have that awful Mr. Roosevelt Mrs. Lundbeck loves so much to thank for it."

Teddy thought it was the longest thing anybody had ever said to him in his whole life. Then she turned back to Grandpa Schroeder.

"Say, if you don't call the police, I'll have to do it myself, upset as I am," she said. "There you are just staring out the window with a pipe in your mouth while your son is about to go to the poor house."

She dabbed at her eyes with a very small white handkerchief, but Teddy thought that she felt sorrier about how upset she was than about his father who was on the phone to Perky upstairs.

The poor house. A job in a gas station for his father. Delivering newspapers for him. No more Mrs. Lundbeck. Teddy suddenly realized that maybe these were the things that happened after the last straw. It made him feel perfectly awful. Mrs. Lundbeck said there were people living in piano crates in the Jersey flats, whatever the Jersey flats were. Soon he and Bean would probably be living with them. The whole world was cracking like that bottle in the kitchen the day before. He felt even more scared than he had the time he'd looked back and seen a wave the size of a mountain about to crash down on him.

Mrs. Schroeder had appeared in the doorway. Apparently she had been standing in the hall the whole time.

"I wish you wouldn't say things like that to the children, Mother Schroeder," Teddy heard her saying. He couldn't believe she was so brave. "Things are bad enough as they are without your making them worse." She looked so strong and pretty standing there in her green dress with her hair shiny from brushing.

"Everything is going to work out somehow. It has to," she said. "Ted says Perky thinks those bottles may have gotten damaged in the box somehow, and that's why they broke. I won't have you telling the children all these terrible things."

Teddy wondered if Grandma Schroeder was going to come over and punch his mother for daring to talk to her that way, but she didn't. She dabbed at her eyes a few more times. "I am so nervous about how we're going to get back home that I don't know what I'm saying," she said.

"Ted would like to drive in with you when the time comes," Mrs. Schroeder said. "He has an appointment to talk things over with Perky this afternoon."

"Well, that's the best news I've heard for a long time," Grandpa Schroeder said. He had his pipe between his teeth, and it wobbled up and down as he talked. "Mother will be glad to have his company," he said— Mother was what he usually called Grandma Schroeder—"and God knows so will I."

"Why don't you kids go have breakfast now and go play in the snow." Mrs. Schroeder said. "Daddy says he will come see you before he leaves."

It ended up being the most fun they'd ever had playing in the snow in their lives though it certainly didn't start out that way. At first all they could do was stand out in the driveway with their winter clothes on and think about how awful everything was.

"What's the poor house, Teddy?" Bean asked, and Teddy said he didn't know.

"I just hope it isn't one of those piano crates," she said. "There wouldn't be room for a bed or a radio or anything."

"There wouldn't be any electricity in it

either, stupid," Teddy said, "so what good would a radio do you?" Right away he wished he hadn't called her stupid.

"We could always go live with Dan," he said. "Dan has enough rooms in her house for everybody."

"Mrs. Lundbeck could come with us too," Bean said. "And maybe there are more jobs in Pittsburgh than there are in New York, and Daddy will find one that makes lots of money and not have to work in a gas station the way Grandma said."

"Grandma is the fattest, meanest old cow I've ever known," Teddy said. He had heard his mother call her an old cow.

"I hate her," Bean said. Again Teddy felt sorry he'd said it. She wasn't half as mean as Mr. Schultz and she couldn't help being fat. He knew Bean didn't hate her really, and he didn't either.

"Did you hear what Mommy said about the bottles?" he said. "Maybe the only reason they broke is they got hurt in the box when Daddy was bringing them out."

"Maybe we will be as rich as Grandpa and Grandma someday," Bean said.

"Someday we will," Teddy said.

"I don't feel like sledding, do you?" Bean said.

"I don't feel like it either."

"What'll we do then," Bean said.

It was a gray cloudy day and already the snow had begun to melt a little. Every once in a while a piece of it would drop from the branches of the trees. The plow had finished scraping the driveway clear and gone away. There were bits of gravel embedded in the banks like raisins where the tracks of the plow had thrown them up. The pile of snow by the garage was even higher than when the children had first seen it from their window. The man who ran the plow had left a snow shovel sticking in it when he had finished shoveling away in front of the garage doors.

"I'll tell you what we can do," Teddy said. "We can make an igloo right there." He pointed to the big pile. "We can dig a hole and hollow it out inside and make a regular snow house."

It took them most of the morning, and they had more fun doing it than almost anything else they had ever done in their lives. The hardest part was getting it started. The snow on the outside of the pile was hard and lumpy where the blade of the plow had kept on banging up against it, and it was partly frozen too. Teddy had to chop at it again and again to work a piece loose and then they would get down on their knees and pull it away with their hands so Teddy could go on and chop out another one. Finally they got enough of it out of the way, though, to expose the snow underneath, and that was much easier to work with. In fact it was still so fluffy and light there that they didn't even have to use the shovel any more. All they had to do was burrow at it with their hands and before long they had a hole big enough for both of them to crawl into at once.

Snow had gotten into their galoshes and down inside their sweaters by then, but it didn't bother them. They burrowed in further and further and then they started scooping it out inside to make it bigger, scraping away at the low ceiling and clawing away at the narrow walls until finally it was big enough for them both to kneel in without bumping their heads. After a while there was room enough for them even to move around a little, and then they started patting the walls and ceiling with the flat of their hands to make them hard and clearing out the loose snow left over from the digging. By the time they finished you still had to get down on your hands and knees to crawl in through the door, but then once you were in, Teddy thought it was the most magic place he had ever seen.

It was very white and cold enough to see your breath in, but it seemed warmer than it was outside and the still air had a lovely secret feeling to it. There were places where you could see the daylight through the snow walls, and everything had a sort of silvery look to it like a palace of ice in one of the Oz books that Teddy couldn't remember the name of just then.

He and Bean were just sitting there all shivery and wide-eyed and looking around at the unbelievable thing they had made when the light that came in through the entrance hole was suddenly blocked off and the next thing they knew they saw their father come crawling through it to be with them. It was pretty crowded by the time he got all the way in, but by sitting with their knees tucked under their chins there was room for all three of them.

Mr. Schroeder had on his city overcoat and muffler but instead of the fedora he usually wore he'd put on a funny looking wool cap he used sledding sometimes that had a green pom-pom on it as big as a tennis ball.

"Hi, kids," he said. "This is some igloo you've got here."

126

They could see the little puffs of his breath as he talked and even in the cold, still air they could smell the smell of him, which was part shaving soap and part tobacco. His eyes glistened and he blew on his bare hands to warm them.

"I've got to leave with Grandpa and Grandma now. You know how Grandma is about waiting," he said. "I've come to say goodbye."

They showed him how they'd patted the walls and ceiling to make them smooth and the places where the daylight shone through and told him what a job they'd had getting the hard part chopped out with the shovel. He looked at all of it very carefully, and they could tell he thought it was pretty good.

"You two are something all right," he said. "I'm very proud of you."

"We're going to make it still bigger," Teddy said.

"Do you think everything would melt if we made just a tiny little fire in the corner?" Bean said.

"Listen, kids," Mr. Schroeder said. "I've got to skedaddle. Teddy, you take good care of Mommy when I'm gone. I mean if she has trouble getting things done, you give her a hand. This is such a busy time with Christmas coming and everything. And Bean, you help too. I know you will, both of you. You're wonderful kids and you always have been. Whatever you do, don't ever be anything else. And don't forget how much I love you either."

"When are you coming back, Daddy?" Teddy said.

"Supper," Mr. Schroeder said. "If nothing happens bigger than a woodchuck, I ought to be back in plenty of time for supper."

He wasn't back for supper.

Many hours had gone by since Teddy and Bean had stood on top of their igloo waving at their grandparents' long black car as it drove slowly out of the driveway, Mr. Schroeder in front with Paul and their grandparents all bundled up with a fur rug over their knees in back.

It had gotten dark, and Mrs. Lundbeck said supper would be ruined if they waited much longer. Mrs. Schroeder stood by the living room window smoking one cigarette after another. She called up the Schroeders in New York to see if they could tell her anything, but Grandma Schroeder said they had let Mr. Schroeder off at the Grand Central Building and thought he would have been home long ago.

It was almost nine o'clock when the telephone rang. Mrs. Schroeder ran past the charcoal man on his horse to answer it upstairs. From the hallway below, they could hear her talking and she didn't talk long. In a few minutes after they heard her hang up, she came down. She got about half way, and then she stopped and sat down right there on the stairs.

"Teddy, Bean," she said. "I've got something I have to tell you."

There was a splintery spot on the step she was sitting on where Mrs. Lundbeck must have nicked it carrying up the carpet sweeper. She reached out with one finger to smooth it down.

"Daddy has had an accident," she said. "He was running to catch the subway apparently. He must have tripped. Or maybe somebody shoved him by mistake. Those subway crowds are so awful. He fell on the tracks before anybody could get to him."

"What do you mean, Mommy?" Teddy said.

"I mean Daddy was killed, darling," Mrs. Schroeder said. "He fell on the tracks just as the subway was coming and there wasn't time to get him out of the way and he was killed."

Even on days when things like that happen, people finally have to go to bed just the way they do on days when nothing much has happened. Teddy climbed in the way he always did. He pulled the covers up over his shoulders and squirmed around trying to get comfortable. First he lay on one side and then he lay on the other. He used only one pillow because his father had told him that two would make him round-shouldered, but just one didn't seem enough just then, so he shoved his arm in under it to make it higher. As he did so, he felt something hard and cold under his hand, the way the keys had felt that awful night in Sagapac. Only it wasn't keys.

When he pulled it out, he found that it was his father's gold watch, the one with the gold chain attached to it and the fancy initials on the back.

ten

They listened to the king's speech on Bean's Mickey Mouse radio, except that he wasn't the king any more because he had given that up so he could marry skinny, black-haired Mrs. Simpson. It was getting on toward Christmas, and some of the children in Teddy's class went around singing "Hark the herald angels sing, Mrs. Simpson stole our king." Teddy thought he sounded on the radio a lot the way he looked—puzzled and sad, as if even now that the unpleasant thing he had been dreading so long had finally happened, he didn't quite know what to make of it.

He spoke in an old man's voice, with one of the tubes in Bean's radio rattling every time he hit a certain note, and said that the reason he'd given up being king was that he couldn't handle the job any more without Mrs. Simpson. Bean felt very sorry for him because he didn't have a castle to live in now or a crown to wear or anything like that.

Teddy felt sorry for him too, but he said that at least it was his own idea. Nobody told him he couldn't be king any more. He himself was the one who had decided it, so at least it was what he wanted and that made it all right.

Uncle Don came on soon after the speech was over. He started talking about his puddle jumper and Susan Beduzen and how all the girls and boys should send in for their banks and become Earnest Savers, and Teddy and Bean soon forgot all about Mrs. Simpson and the rest of it. They both of them thought that Uncle Don was sort of stupid, but they liked listening to him anyway.

They were all very busy getting ready to leave New Jersey for good. Although the lease on the house ran out on the first of the year, the lady who rented it to them— the one who had drawn the man on the horse—said they could keep on living there free until she found somebody else to rent it if they wanted to. But Mrs. Schroeder didn't want to. She decided it would be better to leave as soon as they could get everything done that needed to be done.

She never had liked the house much anyway and especially not *now*, she said. She didn't talk about what she meant by *now*, and the children didn't talk about it either. In fact they didn't talk about anything they thought would upset her or make her sad because that made them sad too. Even when they were alone together in their room, they hardly ever talked about it. The few times they did they used the word *now* too.

"Do you think Mrs. Lundbeck will go on working for us now?" Bean asked.

"I guess now," Teddy said, "lots of things will be different."

Mrs. Schroeder decided that after they left New Jersey they would go stay with Dan in Pittsburgh for a while until they could figure out what they ought to do next. They would leave in time to get there for Christmas, and in the meanwhile they had to take care of all the things you have to take care of when you move. They had moved enough times before so Teddy and Bean didn't think all that much about it. Mrs. Schroeder tried to sell the Pierce Arrow, but it was so old and sick that nobody wanted it so she finally told the junk man that if he would come and tow it away she would let him have it for nothing. She told him he could also have the old second-hand piano in the cellar that they had bought for Teddy to have lessons on before they decided they couldn't afford to, but the junk man said he would be willing to pay for that and gave her a check for ten dollars.

Most of the furniture wasn't theirs so they didn't have to worry about that, and the few things that were theirs Mrs. Schroeder put in storage. One of them was a little desk she'd had when she was Bean's age, and the other was her dressing table that had a mirror on it that she had painted herself with the French words, *Il faut souffrir pour être belle*, which she said meant, "You have to suffer to be beautiful."

There were also certain other things, clothes mostly, that had to be given away because in the first place nobody would have probably thought they were good enough to pay money for and in the second place even if they had thought so, Mrs. Schroeder said, she would rather just let people who needed them have them. She asked Mrs. Lundbeck to take care of it for her, and Mrs. Lundbeck got some people from the Salvation Army to come over one afternoon to take them away while Mrs. Schroeder went with Teddy and Bean to the movies so she wouldn't have to be there when they did it.

Just before they were ready to go, Mrs. Schroeder sent her wardrobe trunk and a few big boxes full of linen and summer clothes ahead by railway express, and the rest they managed to get either into the trunk of the good car or onto a rack that Mrs. Schroeder had to buy especially for the trip. Grandma Schroeder lent them Paul for a day, and he came out from the city one morning to install it for them and put the luggage on it and then lash it down with clothesline so it wouldn't blow off on the road once they got going.

Mrs. Schroeder had to tell Mrs. Lundbeck that she couldn't afford to pay her salary any more, but Mrs. Lundbeck said she would come and help get them settled in Pittsburgh anyway if they wanted her to, and of course they did. So the four of them made the long drive to Pennsylvania together. Teddy and Mrs. Schroeder sat in the front seat and Mrs. Lundbeck and Bean sat in back with a few of the squishier bags tucked in around them and under their feet. The big tunnels through the Allegheny Mountains hadn't been built yet so they had to take the very steep, winding roads that went right over the top of them, and Teddy kept the map open on his lap so he could tell his mother which road went to Pittsburgh when she wasn't sure.

They arrived at Dan's house not long before Christmas, and of all the houses they had ever known, it was the one that Teddy and Bean liked best. One reason they did was that all the time they had spent moving from one place to the other, it was the one house that always stayed the same and that they had kept coming back to for as long as they could remember. The other reason they liked it best was just that it was so wonderful.

It was three stories high with a terrace that ran all along the front of it and a lot of steep green lawn all around it and a long white garage out behind it that could have held six cars easily and had once been a stable in the days before cars were invented. When you came through the front door into the hall, there was a big living room on the left and a big library on the right, and of course it was the library that was Teddy's favorite because of all the books in it. Most of them were in book cases with glass doors to them, and some of the ones he especially liked were the Andrew Lang fairy tale books that Dan had bought for Mrs. Schroeder when she was little. There was the *Red Fairy Tale Book* and the Blue one, the Lavender one, the Yellow one, and so on, and each was bound in the right color with pictures stamped on the cover in gold and very complicated, grown-up-looking black-and-white illustrations inside.

There was a wide white staircase that started in the hallway and went up to a landing and then changed direction and went up to the second floor where the bedrooms were and then on up again to the third floor. The maids' rooms were up there and all sorts of other rooms, some of which didn't have much in them except for a few dead flies on the window sills and others that were full of empty suitcases and boxes of things that nobody used any more. If you stood at the very top of the staircase on the third floor and looked down to the bottom, it seemed almost as high as Grandma and Grandpa Schroeder's apartment in New York, and you could see the bald spots on people's heads and the queer footless way they seemed to move around when you looked straight down on them like that.

There were fireplaces in all the bedrooms, only instead of having andirons in them for burning logs they had little standing asbestos grates that looked like washboards and ran on gas. Before Teddy and Bean got up in the mornings, Ellen, the maid, came in to start them. First they would hear the hiss of the gas, then the scratch of the wooden match as she struck it on the box, and then the little pah! as the gas caught fire. Once it was going, the flames made a soft, fluttery sound as they went rippling over and over up the asbestos.

It was too cold to use the sleeping porch, so Teddy and Bean lived in a room with a bay window in it. There were several other rooms with bay windows too, and there was one little bit of a balcony just big enough to get a suntan on in the summer, and underneath the sleeping porch there was the screened-in kitchen porch sticking out and the dormer windows on the third floor and so on and so forth so that from behind Teddy thought it looked like a great sprawling castle with battlements and green shutters and places where it could have stood a fresh coat of white paint.

Dan's real name was Mrs. Shoemaker, and Mr. Shoemaker was the only one of the children's grandparents they didn't have any nickname or shortened name for like Grandpa but called just plain Grandfather because that was what he was. He was a tall man with a close-cropped moustache instead of a drooping one like Grandpa Schroeder's. He also had blue eyes and over one eyebrow a round pink mole about the size of a pea. He was completely bald except for a gray fringe around the edges. A lot of the time he was rather quiet and shy, but sometimes he would get into a jolly mood and not be shy at all. One of the things he would do then was call almost everybody Peter. He called them that whether it happened to be their name or not. Sometimes he called Teddy and Bean Peter. Sometimes he called Mrs. Schroeder Peter. The only person he never called Peter was Dan, and he called her either Dear or Margaret, which was her true first name. She told him he was not to pronounce it Mar-gret as if it was only two syllables long but Mar-gar-et so people could hear that it was three.

Sometimes when he was not feeling jolly he could get very cross, and one of the things that made him crossest was peanut butter. He said he had never tasted it but knew he would hate it if he did. He also hated the way it looked. Most of all he hated the smell of it. If Teddy and Bean wanted peanut butter and jelly sandwiches for lunch, he would make them go eat out in the kitchen, and if he happened to forget and wander in while they were doing it, he would get out in a hurry. Another thing he hated was marbles or beads or any small round things the children might leave lying around on the floor, and another was any mixture of foods like succotash or carrots and peas served together in the same dish or omelets that had anything inside them except eggs.

When the children and Mrs. Schroeder first arrived with all their luggage on top of the car and Mrs. Lundbeck in the back seat and everything else, he didn't say anything about what had made them decide to leave New Jersey for good and come there. He just kissed his daughter on her forehead and shook Teddy and Bean by their hands and said, "Well!"

"Well," he said, "Well," and each of the three or four times he said it, it had a different sound to it as if it meant three or four different things that he couldn't find any other way of saying.

Dan didn't say anything about why they had decided to come either, at least not then, but although she wasn't a kissy person like Grandma Schroeder, she kissed both Teddy and Bean as well as her daughter and gave them tighter and longer hugs than they could remember her ever having given them before.

Mrs. Lundbeck said she would stay

through New Year's, and the room she had was on the third floor right next to Ellen's. Ellen had a long, thin nose and red hair and would have died rather than paint her eyebrows on even if she'd needed to, but she and Mrs. Lundbeck seemed to get on very well together anyhow, which was just as well, Dan said, because they had to use the same bathroom and if they had taken a dislike to each other, that might have made things unpleasant.

Whenever Mrs. Lundbeck went to a new city, she always liked to spend her first day off going to visit the slums so she could see how the poor people lived and what good things President Roosevelt was doing to help them. She asked Ellen to tell her where the slums of Pittsburgh were, but Ellen didn't know. She said she thought the poor people probably just lived any place where they could find a roof over their heads. So when Mrs. Lundbeck's first day off came, which was always a Thursday, she set out to find the slums all by herself and didn't return till so long after supper that Ellen was quite worried about her. When she finally did return, everybody could see right away that she had lost her false teeth. She never explained how she had lost them any more than she ever explained why she wouldn't put her dime in the conductor's machine on the Fifth Avenue bus, but Dan said she bet she could make a good guess.

"The poor soul probably found herself in some rundown neighborhood and wondered if it was what she was looking for," Dan said. "Then she probably went up to some respectable citizen who happened to have been born and bred there and his father before him and asked him politely if these were the slums of Pittsburgh and he was so insulted that he laid hands upon her. I'll bet you a dollar I'm right," Dan said, and both the children agreed that she probably was. Fortunately Mrs. Lundbeck had a spare set of teeth, which needed only a little adjusting, so she was all right again in just a few days.

In some ways of course it wasn't exactly a merry Christmas.

"I know you'll understand, kids," Mrs. Schroeder said once. "I just can't do the kind of things that we did before."

Before was another word like *now* and *well* that you could use for getting certain things across without having to make people sad by coming right out and saying them. It seemed queer to Teddy at first to have things as big as that and never talk about them but by not

142

talking about them himself either, he stopped thinking about them so much, and after a while there were days when he almost forgot that they had happened at all.

One afternoon when it was raining he found Bean sitting underneath the bridge table in their room with her Mickey Mouse radio playing on top of it and tears running down through her freckles. When he asked her what in the world she was so sad about, she looked up at him with a very fierce expression on her face.

"*You* know why," she said. "*You* know," and then suddenly of course he did know and thought how sad and awful it was that at first he hadn't.

Almost always—before—they had gone to have Christmas Day with Grandma and Grandpa Schroeder in their apartment in New York. Their uncles and aunts and cousins would all be there too, and Rosa would come and hang up everybody's coat in the closet, and then they would all wait in the large, dark hall for the signal to open the curtained glass doors and go into the living room where the tree and the presents were. The signal was the ringing of a big bell like the kind that Salvation Army Santa Clauses use on street corners, and the person who had the job of ringing it was Grandpa Schroeder. Then the doors would open and everybody would rush in.

All around the living room the presents were piled, and each of the children had a pile with his or her name on it, and there were so many of them to open that it would go on for hours while the grown-ups sat around smoking and laughing and talking and having their cocktails. The tree had real candles on it, and the whole time they were lit a nephew of Rosa and Anna's named Kurt, who was a policeman, would be hired for the day to stand near it with a bucket of water so he could quickly put them out in case the tree caught fire.

Dan also had a tree for them, of course, though she had electric lights on it instead of real candles. She had it set up in the library, which was a good place for it because when the lights were on, you could see them reflected in the glass doors of all the bookcases and it looked as if there were about a hundred times as many. Naturally there were presents too, though not nearly as many as the Schroeders had in New York. Mr. Shoemaker had put a lot of money into an oil well that turned out not to have any oil in it so he wasn't as rich any more as the children's other grandparents were and besides it cost a lot to run the big house. But even when he and Dan had been richer, they never went in for such piles of presents as the Schroeders.

The Shoemakers opened their presents on Christmas Eve instead of the next morning. They did it after supper with just the tree and a few candles on the mantlepiece to light the library, and the asbestos fire rippling in the fireplace. Ellen brought in a big silver bowl of eggnog made with real cream and lots of egg whites beaten stiff with an eggbeater, and they all had some including Teddy and Bean who each had one cup with a sprinkling of nutmeg floating on the top. Mr. Shoemaker called Mrs. Lundbeck Peter for the first time when she and Ellen came in to get their presents, and Teddy sang "Hark the herald angels sing, Mrs. Simpson stole our king" for them and everybody laughed.

Dan gave Mrs. Schroeder a blue silk Chinese mandarin's coat with a shell pink lining and embroidered all over with little flowers and birds, and she put it right on and sat by the fire in it having her eggnog. She was rather quiet at first, but she then she got to talking about other Christmases she'd had in that very same room when she and her sister were children. For the first time that Teddy and Bean had heard her do it in a long while she laughed when Dan reminded her how on one particular Christmas she had taken over the tea set that had been her younger sister Ruth's main present—Ruth was the sister Bean had been named for—and how proud Ruth had been just to be allowed to use the cream pitcher.

Then they got all bundled up in their winter clothes and started off for the midnight service at a big stone church that wasn't very far away. Dan didn't usually go to it because of the way her stomach rumbled and Mr. Shoemaker always said he was too busy trying to keep the wolf away from the door, but it was mostly carols, Dan said, instead of a lot of kneeling down and standing up and apologizing to God about what miserable sinners they were, and she thought the children would enjoy it.

It was snowing when they got there—not a heavy snow like the one on Thanksgiving Day but just a lazy scattering of flakes that glittered like stars when they fell through the light of the street lamps. When people first came in, they still had a dusting of them on their hats and on the fur collars of their coats.

The church was so filled that they were lucky to find a pew with room enough in it for all five of them to sit together. It was way down in front near where the manger was. Around the manger there were quite a few life-sized wooden figures dressed up in real clothes. Joseph and Mary were closest to it, Mary dressed in the same color blue as Mrs. Schroeder's Chinese coat and Joseph standing just beside her looking down. The three kings were there too, of course, with different kinds of crowns on their heads. There were two white kings and one black one, and the shorter of the two white ones had a drooping moustache, which made Bean whisper to Teddy that he looked exactly like Grandpa Schroeder. There were a couple of kneeling shepherds too and a few animals standing around in the real straw. The children couldn't see into the manger because one of the shepherds' heads was in the way, but they could see that it was lined with more of the real straw and there was a soft white light shining up out of it that lit Mary's face from underneath the way Rosa's face had been lit up when she carried in Teddy's birthday cake.

The service began with everybody standing up while the choir marched in holding candles and singing "Hark the Herald Angels Sing," which made Dan turn around and give Teddy her riverboat gambler look. Then the minister stood up in a pulpit with a roof on it which Teddy whispered to Bean looked like the orange juice squeezer they had had in New Jersey. He was a short man who wore glasses with steel rims, which flickered in the light whenever he moved his head, and he read some of the parts of the Bible that have to do with Christmas, ending with the story about the shepherds keeping watch over their flocks by night and how the kings were guided to the manger by a star. He read from the Bible in a voice that sounded pretty much like everybody else's, but when he said the prayer at the end Teddy could hear right away that he was saying it in a begging voice.

Then they all sat down and sang a lot of carols. The ushers passed out little paper books that had all the words in them, and Teddy and Bean used one together, each holding one side of it. They sang "Silent Night" and "O Come All Ye Faithful" and "O Little Town of Bethlehem" and "It Came upon a Midnight Clear." Then the choir got up and sang something that didn't sound much like Christmas at all and had one very high part in it that was sung by a woman with the same kind of rouge spots on her cheeks that Mrs. Lundbeck sometimes put on for her Thursdays off. There were some more carols after that including "Good King Wenceslas" and "God Rest Ye Merry Gentlemen," and then when the plate had been passed and the minister had said a few more things, he raised his arms in the air with his glasses shining and said one last thing, and then everybody got up and started putting on their coats to go home.

Teddy and Bean were so tired by the time they got into bed that they could hardly get undressed. They talked a little bit about the presents they had gotten and the king that looked like Grandpa Schroeder and the way Grandfather Shoemaker had put a whole five dollar bill in the plate to be for all of them. They wondered if there would be as much snow on the ground when they woke up the next morning as there had been in New Jersey. Teddy was going to say something about the igloo and how all three of them had been able to fit in it together for a few minutes, but then he didn't.

They were just about to put out the light

when Bean asked Teddy if he remembered which of the carols it was that had the part about the beach in it.

"The beach!" Teddy said. "Christmas carols aren't about beaches, dopey."

"This one was," Bean said.

"Maybe the eggnog made you drunk," he said.

"No, it didn't," she said.

They lay there for a while without saying anything, and then Teddy reached over to the lamp that was on the table between their beds.

"Wait a sec," Bean said. She jumped out of bed and went over to the bureau. "I'll show you the one I mean right here in the book."

It was the little book of carols they had been given in church, and she held it under the lamp and turned the pages over one by one. She did it again only more slowly this time, running her stubby finger down each page as she came to it. She had a piece of her hair in the corner of her mouth and was chewing on it as she searched.

"There!" she said finally and stuck the book practically under Teddy's nose. "It's "God Rest Ye Merry Gentleman," the very last verse. Read it yourself if you think I'm such a dope."

Teddy took it out of her hand and read it, and this is what it said:

Now to the Lord sing prais-es,
    All you with-in this place,
And with true love and broth-er-hood
    Each oth-er now em-brace;
This ho-ly tide of Christ-mas
    Doth bring re-deem-ing grace.
O ti-dings of com-fort and joy,
    com-fort and joy;
O ti-dings of com-fort and joy!

He read it through a couple more times, and while he was reading it and for a little bit afterward he thought a lot of thoughts all at once as Bean sat there on the edge of her bed chewing on her hair and waiting for him to say something.

He wasn't sure what the word *tide* meant in the song—only that it didn't have any-thing to do with the beach the way Bean had thought—but he couldn't help thinking about the beach anyway. He thought about the one at Sagapac and how his father had told him that when you ride the waves, you should remember that they want to get you

151

safely back to shore just the way you want to yourself. He thought about the undertow too—the sea puss as Dan had called it—and how it could drag you out to sea the other way if you weren't careful. But the waves were stronger, Dan said, and no matter how far the low tide goes out, the high tide always comes in again as high as ever.

Of course he thought about his father too and how he had swum him on his shoulders out to the barrels that time. He thought about how terrible it was that nobody ever talked about him any more so that it was almost as if there had never been any such person. He decided that from now on he wanted to talk about him a lot. He wanted to remember everything about him that he could remember so someday he could tell about him to other people who had never even seen him. He wanted to remember how his father had slipped the gold watch under his pillow that morning as a goodbye present because he had known what he was going to do when he got to the city just the way King Edward had known what he was going to do when he couldn't stand being king any more. He had done it because he had had to do it, so it was all right.

Then Bean couldn't bear to wait any longer.

"What is the tide of Christmas then if you think you're so smart?" she said.

Teddy put the book down on the table between their beds.

"It's the high tide, Bean," he said. "It's the Wizard of Oz tide. It's the one that brings you home."

"Everybody?" Bean said.

"Everybody," Teddy said.

Then he said just one more thing even though he nearly didn't because he was afraid it might make Bean cry the way she had been crying the time he found her under the bridge table.

"Even Daddy," he said.

It didn't make her cry at all. She got back into bed and pulled the covers up so that not much more than her topknot was sticking out. Then Teddy turned the light off at last, and they lay there in the dark without saying anything for a little while. Then they fell fast asleep without even bothering to talk about Miss Lilywhite's party and who they hoped they would find when they got there.